WIND RIDER

The Sioux call him Wind Rider . . . Hank Benteen rides into trouble in a Wyoming valley after saving the lives of a homesteader and his children. A range war is brewing and some of the cowboys are hiding a murderous secret. Then, resolving to safeguard the homesteaders' properties, Benteen becomes involved in a deadly game with two avaricious men, intent on acquiring land by brute force. The Wind Rider will need all his skills as a gunman to survive . . .

THOMAS McNULTY

WIND RIDER

Complete and Unabridged

LINFORD
Leicester

First published in Great Britain in 2010 by
Robert Hale Limited
London

First Linford Edition
published 2011
by arrangement with
Robert Hale Limited
London

The moral right of the author has been asserted

British Library CIP Data

McNulty, Thomas, *1955* –
Wind rider. - -
(Linford western library)
1. Ranchers- -Fiction. 2. Western stories.
3. Large type books.
I. Title II. Series
813.6–dc22

ISBN 978–1–4448–0683–0

Published by
F. A. Thorpe (Publishing)
Anstey, Leicestershire

Set by Words & Graphics Ltd.
Anstey, Leicestershire
Printed and bound in Great Britain by
T. J. International Ltd., Padstow, Cornwall

This book is printed on acid-free paper

Dedicated to Steve Hayes
Thanks for leading the way

1

The air was crisp and he smelled smoke when he rode into the valley. His name was Hank Benteen but the Sioux called him Wind Rider. He was fifty-two years old, tall but lean, and he possessed no skills other than those that come from being a cowpuncher. Everything he owned he wore or was to be found in his saddle-bags. None of the big cities was to his liking and he never lasted long in small towns. His hair was long and bleached by the sun.

He rode without direction until he smelled the smoke. He was a two days' ride from Jackson Hole when he crested a ridge, reined his horse and gazed across a plain of sage and tall grass. He marveled at the rolling hills and distant mountains that fell across the horizon like the purple shadow of a fallen giant.

He stretched, straightened his legs in the stirrups. Since he'd left South Dakota he'd been debating where to go next. He'd been down in Cheyenne the year before and he had a hankering to roam Wyoming's vast landscape. He patted his horse, an old paint.

'We'll follow the smoke,' he said to his horse. 'I guess that'll do.'

Hank Benteen had keen eyes and an intuitive mind. Wandering was his skill. He possessed the ability to drift without purpose or until a purpose found him. He could read trails better than most; an abandoned campfire easily gave up its secrets to his sharp eyes. He understood the signs and pieced his assumptions together intuitively. That was how he drifted into situations that gave him his reputation.

He could never stay long in one place. A few months at the most and then he was riding again. He most often worked for ranchers as a cowpuncher, riding fence lines or rounding up strays. He seldom worked at one place for more than one season. Men spoke his name with respect, but with caution, too.

When the sky changed to twilight it reminded him of his home he'd left behind at the age of twelve. He thought wistfully about his father's ranch in Oklahoma. In the early evening he would sit with his pa on the porch talking. All of that was a long time ago and the memory pained him. He wished the old man was still alive.

He rode into a grove of pine trees near a stream and made camp. He made a fire and cooked some beans and chewed some beef jerky. He could still smell smoke but it wasn't as strong.

He had an idea that he might get a job in Jackson Hole. He needed money to buy supplies so that he could purchase enough provisions to last several weeks. If he could get the money together he could hunt in the mountains for a few weeks and secure some bear furs for trading. Then he thought he might ride to California. He'd never been to California and he had nothing better to do.

Towns had a way of fencing a man in and that wasn't natural, he thought. But he would have to put up with people in Jackson Hole long enough where staying out of trouble might be difficult.

'Nothing to it,' he said to himself. Benteen knew he was a damn fool to be talking to himself.

He pulled out his bedroll and crawled under the blankets. He felt the day's ride sink into his muscles and his body began to relax. He heard his horse, tethered near by, shift its weight and begin nibbling at some tall grass. His right hand dropped to his holster, his fingers tracing the scars along the walnut grip of his Colt.

The night closed in on him. Couple of days from now, he was thinking as sleep took him, I'll get a job in Jackson Hole. He pulled his battered Stetson over his eyes.

'Stop talking to yourself,' he said, and then he fell asleep.

4

But his dreams were troubled. Something rushed past him in the dark and he heard the rattle of bones. He saw again the face of an Apache boy whom he had killed in Arizona. The Apache had been hunting him for three days and his final life-saving advantage had been the dried beef jerky in his saddle-bags. He had sustained his strength while the Apache had gone without food. When they fought in a dry arroyo Benteen had overpowered the wiry youth, clubbed him into a senseless stupor with his fists before drawing his Colt and shooting him. He had not wanted to take the boy's life but he was left with no choice. Had he let the Apache live he would have hunted him again. Now the boy visited him in his dreams and without understanding it his mind mourned the violence that had become a part of his life.

He woke once during the night. The stars were sharp as knives and a gentle breeze brushed across the trees. He

5

tried to remember the sound of his father's voice but it was lost to him. Near dawn he fell into a slumber and for a moment at least the demons of his past allowed him a moment's rest.

When he next opened his eyes morning had arrived like a pale ghost. The sky was slate and the night breeze had died away. He smelled smoke and without thinking about it he had risen and saddled his horse. He followed a dry creek up through the sage and in the distance he saw a tendril of smoke dance in the air.

Thirty minutes later he could make out the charred remains of a cabin. When he was closer still he saw the burned frame of a Morgan wagon and a dead horse.

Benteen didn't have to be told what happened. He recognized from long experience and accepted what had happened. This was cattle country and a homesteader had fenced off a parcel of land and set down roots. This would have been an angry cattleman's mark.

The Homestead Act of 1862 had made it possible to promote settlement in the West, but the cattlemen who had previously enjoyed the benefits of public domain territory that had been open range were resisting the encroachment of these sodbusters, as they called them. After the Civil War the West saw numerous migrations of homesteaders and by 1880 the conflict was near epic proportions in some parts of the country.

Benteen had known and worked for cattlemen and knew most of them were fair and decent-minded men. But there were always those who wanted to settle things with violence. It needled him as he nudged his horse for a closer look.

He found the woman's body near an area that must have been a garden. Some vegetable plants had been pulled out and the ground trampled by a horse. She was red-haired and held a Sharps rifle in her hands. A bullet had marked her brow, just over her left eye.

The ugly wound stood out in contrast to her beauty.

Someone had killed a woman. The fact astonished and horrified him.

He felt a flash of anger coil inside him like a rattlesnake. There would need to be a reckoning for this. Dormant emotions welled up inside him and for a moment he couldn't move, his jaw tightly locked and his teeth clenched together as he fought to keep himself in check.

The man was thirty feet away, lying against the smoking ruins. He was still alive. He was armed with a Colt and Benteen noted the cylinder was empty. The fire had burned part of his shoulder. There was blood on his shirt. Benteen pulled a Bowie knife and cut away the man's shirt. A bullet had taken him on the left side below the ribs. The exit wound was clean but it was unknown what damage the bullet might have caused to his internal organs. At a glance Benteen thought the sodbuster might be lucky. If the bullet had missed the vital organs there was a chance he'd recover. Still, it was a small chance.

Benteen touched the man's forehead. His flesh was warm either from a fever or the fire. He lifted him carefully and set him out under a pine tree. He would have shade here most of the afternoon. Then Benteen went to work cleaning the wound. He used all of the water in his canteen to wipe it out and refilled the canteen in a nearby creek.

He bandaged the wound using one of his own spare shirts from his saddle-bag. The wound was packed with a fine layer of cold mud from the creekside. He would have to change and clean it daily but it offered the man his best chance for survival. Without proper medicine and the care of a doctor Benteen's frontier remedy would have to do.

Once the man regained consciousness and stared at Benteen.

'Who are you?' he asked, his voice faltering.

'I found you a little while ago,'

Benteen said. 'I was riding to Jackson Hole. Someone hurt you bad, mister.'

The man's eyes swept past Benteen to the body of his wife lying near the garden. Hank followed the man's gaze then looked back at him and said, 'I'll give her a proper burial. Then when you're better we'll find out who did this.'

The man nodded weakly and Benteen knew he was committed even before he said the words. He had ridden with the wind a long time and he would make the reckoning with his gun.

The man tried to sit up but Benteen held his palm against his shoulder. 'Ease up. You need to rest.'

The man opened his mouth and said, 'The girls . . . ' but he had lost too much blood. He closed his eyes and slipped into unconsciousness again.

Benteen set to burying the woman. He found a shovel with a charred handle but usable. He chose a place between a grove of trees and began turning up the earth. He removed his shirt, folded it and set it carefully on the ground. He unhooked his gunbelt and placed it with his shirt and within easy reach. It was a warm day and the sweat glistened across his torso but he kept a steady pace. The soil turned easily and his hands were blackened by the charred handle.

It took him two hours of steady work to dig a six-foot grave. Then he went to the small creek, removed his boots, and waded into the cold water. The flow from the spring thaw in the Big Horn mountains added ice to the creek and he scrubbed himself clean. The sun would dry his trousers in a few minutes.

He examined the burned cabin and sifted through the timbers looking for something that might serve as a shroud. He didn't want to put the woman in the ground without a shroud. It wasn't right. All of the linen had burned but as he stood in the shattered doorway something nagged him. He couldn't quite place it and stood silently a moment thinking.

The sod roof had fallen at an eastern angle and made a pile of grass and timbers. This side of the cabin had suffered the least amount of damage. The attacker or attackers had not done an adequate job with the fire. While most of the cabin burned there was enough of the frame still standing so that a reconstruction would be easier than if it had all burned to ash.

The floor was intact along with a good portion of the southern wall. Most of the furniture had burned but Benteen could make out the remains of a dresser and table. It had been a big cabin and enormous effort had gone into its construction. The man must have had help which meant other homesteaders were in the area. They usually settled in groups in spacious territory. The house had been built high and at the periphery of a pine grove. Benteen knew there was something he should be looking at but it eluded him.

He decided he would have to bury

the woman in one of his two Mexican blankets. It was his only logical choice and he felt it was the right thing to do. Later, he would explain to the man what he had done and apologize for not being able to do better. Benteen knew the choices were not his fault but his own code demanded such from him. He took one of the rolled blankets from his saddle.

It was grim work. He gingerly wrapped the woman in the blanket and avoided looking into her face. He carried her to the grave and stepped in, easing her body down gently. He climbed out and wished that he knew words to speak before he slowly began shoveling the earth on to the body. When he was finished he was sweating again and his hands were again blackened by the charred handle but he never could have buried her if he'd hadn't been clean. The dead deserve our respect as much as when they are alive.

Once again he wished he knew words

to speak over the grave but all he could think to say was '*Vaya con Dios*.' It had to be enough.

He used a flat stone about a foot long from the creekbed for a marker. Later the man could have a proper stone set in place.

The sun had begun its descent and Benteen marveled at the beauty of his surroundings. He never tired of the country and these sodbusters had chosen a nice piece of Heaven for themselves. The fading horizon was burning with streaks of orange and the clouds had darkened like cotton dipped in ink. The breeze had picked up and the trees were in constant motion, dancers at twilight who swayed to the beat of ancient songs known only to the Sioux.

He had traveled a long road, propelled by the wind and spurred by his own discontent: a lonely trail that had nearly cost him his life. But he was fast with a gun and he owed his life to Sam Colt and his own uncanny ability to find ways to survive.

The thought that had been nagging at his mind became clear to him. He fixed his gaze on the cabin and thought they would have dug a small cellar. He wanted to retrieve what little of their belongings he could and there might be additional tools that he could salvage. Benteen was of the opinion that nothing went to waste, no matter the circumstances.

He found it under the burned table. He kicked aside the debris and heard a sound like a small animal crying. There was a notch in one of the floorboards that could only have been carved by a man with a knife. And he heard that sound again and he knew immediately there wasn't an animal hiding under the floorboards.

Benteen lifted the boards and in the fading afternoon light he looked into the frightened faces of two little red-headed girls.

2

Rebecca Deloney went to the doorway and watched Mason Shrive walk aimlessly across the street. He kept his head down watching his own feet, which generally meant that he was drunk or still suffering from last night's liquor. She had no sympathy for the man. It was mid-morning but the town of Pitchstone was bustling with activity.

She watched Mason Shrive amble across the street and on to the boardwalk where he leaned against a post and lit a cheroot. He smoked greedily, glancing furtively up the street. The man had been up to no good, of that Rebecca was certain.

Three days ago she had overheard Mason talking with Walt Driggs. The two men worked for Mr Charles Nickles and there was a great deal of talk lately about the homesteaders.

Rebecca heard idle conversation daily at her restaurant, but something in the tone of Mason's voice gave her pause.

'The man can't talk at me that way,' she heard Mason say.

'You gotta have good reason,' Walt said. 'You can't pull a hogleg on a man without a reason.'

Rebecca went about her business serving up coffee as her waitress, Elma, the town spinster, took orders and served food. Rebecca had the best coffee in town and paid a good penny for it from a merchant forty miles west in Jackson Hole. Pitchstone was growing but wasn't as well-known as Jackson Hole. The cattleman Charles Nickles wanted to change that. It was his investments that had formed the nucleus of this out-of-the-way crossroads camp and he wanted nothing more but to see Pitchstone become the center of his own cattle empire.

Pitchstone wasn't even much of a town yet. A livery, one saloon, Rebecca's eatery, a blacksmith, a dry-goods store, a grain warehouse, and a hotel. The street was surrounded by some outlying shacks and outhouses. And all of it was owned by Charles Nickles. As the only other private investor, Rebecca gave Nickles ten per cent of her profit in exchange for what he called 'security'. She didn't like it but Nickles guaranteed her safety, insurance against fire, and a substantial discount on supplies at his dry-goods store. From a business perspective it made perfect sense. All of her savings were tied up in her restaurant and she wondered whether leaving Cheyenne to follow her dream of independence had been a wise move.

When she glanced through her doorway a few minutes later Shrive was coming into the restaurant. A few minutes later he was followed by Walt Driggs and they sat together for their breakfast.

She went about her chores but she couldn't keep her mind off the snippets of conversation she had heard.

'. . . a wagon of Glidden steel barbed wire is what started it,' she heard Shrive say.

'Well it won't happen now. We'll make some money from this yet.'

'It was all that sodbuster's fault.'

'Don't let your temper get the better of you.'

'You know what we have to do.'

At that the men glanced her way. Mason Shrive was not a handsome man but he was imposing. A dark walrus mustache added to his swarthy appearance. His dark eyes blazed at her defiantly.

'Pour the coffee and mind your business, woman,' he said.

She poured the coffee and said to Mason, 'You seem mighty agitated this morning, Mason.'

'It's none of your affair. If you'd like to know what I think about something we can meet after dark. I have plenty I can say to you.' Mason sneered lasciviously when he spoke.

Rebecca laughed at him. 'You don't have anything to say that much interests me. Just make certain you pay your bill before you haul your tired ass out of here.'

Mason shot her a dark glance. 'I don't like being talked to that way.'

She ignored him and turned her attention to the other patrons. She regretted the encounter but Mason had made crude remarks far too often to ignore. His friend, Walt Driggs, was no better. Older but equally ugly, Walt Driggs always looked like a man near death. He had perpetual dark circles under his eyes and an unkempt beard that was surely home to any number of insects or fleas. Rebecca decided that if Walt Driggs had been a dog she would have shot him to end his misery.

When Shrive and Driggs had finished eating they paid her and left. She felt Driggs looking at her. His stare was unclean, like having a dirty rag pressed against her body. She breathed a sigh of relief when they left. They went out on the boardwalk near the saloon to smoke.

They were upset about a family that

had put a claim on some property that bordered the Nickles ranch. The Benson family. They had come into Pitchstone for supplies and Rebecca liked them. Dave and Josephine Benson. Nice folks. The two little girls, Molly and Miranda, were adorable. But ranchers like Charles Nickles couldn't accept that the days of the open range were coming to an end.

Rebecca thought the ranchers had a burr under their saddles for no good reason. Nickles had more property than any rancher in the area, and people like the Bensons were no threat. This was big country and there was room for all of them.

After the lunch rush she spent an hour cleaning the dishes. Afternoons were slow but the place would fill up again for dinner. Elma swept out the dining room and began helping baking pies. Rebecca's peach and apple pies were popular with the cattlemen. Rebecca bought the canned peaches through a dry-goods wholesale outfit in

Jackson Hole. She didn't care for canned food but she admitted it made life easier. She was thinking that pretty soon the whole country would be eating food out of a can when she heard a commotion in the street.

Through the doorway she could see a group of men converging near Walt Driggs and Mason Shrive on the boardwalk.

A tall, weathered man on horseback pulling a travois was coming down the street. The two little Benson girls were up on the saddle with him. The younger, Molly, sat in front and Miranda clung to his back.

Rebecca's heart sank. That something terrible had happened was obvious. That was Dave Benson on the travois. But where was Josephine?

The group of men stepped off the boardwalk and faced the stranger. Driggs looked furious.

'Sodbusters aren't necessarily welcome here.' She thought Mason had spoken.

22

The man on horseback appraised them coolly. He has some backbone, she thought, because there wasn't a glimmer of fear in the man's eyes.

'This man needs medical assistance and his daughters need food and someone to look after them. I'll see to it that that happens.'

'You'll see to it?' Mason was incredulous.

'Don't make me a part of your fight.'

'Listen, mister — '

'The name's Benteen.'

That stopped them and Rebecca saw the surprise in all of their faces.

After a moment Driggs spoke up. 'This man has a bullet wound and I doubt he'll live anyway.'

'You'll see to it that he gets a chance.'

Mason removed the bandanna from around his neck and wiped the sweat off his face.

'Seems I heard of a Benteen. Maybe there's a Wanted poster out on you.'

'There's not.'

'All the same, you can't expect to

ride into town and start barking orders like a bluebelly sergeant. All of this 'I'll see to it' and 'You'll see to it' isn't sensible. Now I suppose you can put that man up at the hotel if you have the money to pay for him, but then there's the funeral expense, and taking care of these girls will cost some money as well.'

Rebecca saw the man squint, shift in his saddle and turn his head briefly. He was sizing up the increasingly hostile crowd. They were all riders for the Nickles ranch.

Without thinking about it she turned on her heel and strode to the back room where she fetched a Winchester from its resting place in the corner near her desk.

What she did next they would talk about for years after.

Out in the street Driggs thumbed his holster's leather loop from his Colt's hammer. Another moment and the first shot would ignite them all. Once that man pulled his gun they would take him down. Rebecca didn't want to think about that, or what would certainly happen to the girls if she didn't act.

She was out the door and striding purposefully into the street. The stranger saw her before the crowd did and in that instant their eyes met. He had to make an instantaneous decision that she meant him no harm. Then he averted his eyes so as not to draw attention to her. She swung up the Winchester and levered a round into the chamber. The metallic ratchet of the gun was incredibly loud in the hot and dusty street. Just as the crowd turned as one, all eyes wide at this unexpected intrusion, she lifted the rifle to her shoulder and fired at Walt Driggs.

The bullet slammed into the dirt near his boot. He cussed, took a step back.

The rifle shot echoed loudly, carried high by the wind.

'I don't want to see any of you go for

a gun.' Her voice was even, fearless, and her eyes told them she meant it. She levered the rifle again, the spent brass spinning free, another round under the cocked hammer.

'Rebecca! There's no call for this . . . '

She swept the rifle across the crowd.

'Shut your mouth, Mason.' Rebecca nearly hissed the words.

The men began to move away. She looked at the man who called himself Benteen.

'Mister, get those girls off that horse and take them back to my place. That's my restaurant back here. Elma will take care of these girls while you come back and we'll take Mr Benson upstairs.'

'Yes ma'am.'

Had Benteen almost smiled?

The men had all taken up positions on the boardwalk, flanking her on both sides of the street. Driggs slouched in a saloon doorway, his face etched with contempt. She looked around for Mason Shrive but he was gone. Why, that man was a stinking coward after

26

all, she thought.

A few moments later Benteen returned and led his horse toward the restaurant. He lifted Dave Benson from the travois and carried him inside. Rebecca eased the hammer down on the Winchester and backed into the doorway. At least fifteen men had watched all this unfold and their expressions told her this was only the beginning.

With Benson inside they were safe. But for how long?

★   ★   ★

The little girls had changed everything. Dave Benson had awakened briefly and thanked Benteen for burying his wife. The sight of his two daughters had lifted his spirits. Then he slipped into unconsciousness again. Bringing them to Pitchstone was a gamble but Benteen had no choice.

Rebecca instructed him to take the man to her room upstairs. She had an extra bed in a smaller adjoining room where the girls could sleep with her. It was crowded but it was manageable.

Elma immediately took the girls under her wing. 'These youngsters need a bath and some food. I'll get the bath going while you fix them something to eat.' Elma glanced at Benteen. She didn't quite know what to think of him. None of them did. But the Benson girls didn't look as frightened now.

'You must be hungry as well,' Rebecca said.

'I could eat. That's kind of you, ma'am.'

'I'm Rebecca Deloney. Please call me Rebecca. I heard you say your name was Benteen.'

'Hank Benteen.'

'Well, Mr Benteen, you may have ridden into a storm, but you saved those girls. That counts for something.'

He followed her downstairs to the kitchen. She made him a steak and gave him a small loaf of fresh bread. He drank coffee afterward and told her about finding the Benson family. When he told her about burying the woman, Josephine, she turned her back on him and wept quietly. He let her have that time, sipping his coffee. When she was finished she wiped her face with a cotton cloth and poured him a fresh cup of coffee.

'What are you going to do now?' she asked.

'What I told those men outside still stands. I'll see to it these people are taken care of. Since there's some resentment here I'll bide my time and make certain there's no interference.'

'I don't understand how you can do that.'

'One thing at a time. Tell me about those men.'

Rebecca told him about the range war that was brewing, how the Nickles riders had been talking angrily about the homesteaders. Benteen listened intently.

After telling him what she knew she took a platter of food to the girls and left Benteen alone. He sipped his coffee and pondered his situation.

A woman out here in this wild territory without a husband and trying to run a business was impressive to him. She had nerve. Then he thought of something else. She reminded him in small ways of his long dead wife. Mary had the same way of brushing her hair from her eyes, the same swaying movement to her hips when she crossed a room. Maybe it was because he hadn't been around a woman in a long time.

Now she had taken sides with a stranger. She knew nothing of him but reacting on instinct she had taken up with him. That would make her situation as a businesswoman all the more dangerous. But Benteen had faced difficult situations before. Maybe he had one more good fight left in him.

There had been a moment just before the war ended when he'd found himself outflanked by a dozen rebels from Alabama. The graycoats had him in a gully, surrounded and low on ammunition. He made it out alive by killing an eager private who wandered too close to his hiding-place. Benteen had donned the weathered gray coat and passed himself off as a Johnny Reb until he could put distance between himself and the Confederates.

This wouldn't be that easy.

Rebecca came back a few moments later and he asked her if he could sleep in the kitchen.

'Of course, but . . . '

'No, I won't be uncomfortable,' he said, anticipating her question. 'And I can watch the door better here.'

Rebecca nodded. 'There's a small corral out back where you can tie you horse. Elma said she'll stay tonight as well. Those men are riled up and it's best that we all stay off the street.'

'I appreciate it, ma'am.'

'Call me Rebecca.'

'Rebecca.' Benteen smiled. Then he went out and took his horse around the building. The street was oddly quiet and the sun was sinking fast beyond the mountains.

With his horse secured he brought in his saddle, his Winchester, Benson's Colt and holster and the Sharps rifle his wife had been holding when she died. The man would want these if he recovered.

Later, Rebecca returned and sat with him at one of the restaurant tables. The room was lit only by a small oil lamp which Benteen had moved to a corner and out of view from anyone looking in the window. Outside, the street was quiet.

'I felt that I should explain myself somewhat,' she began.

'How so?'

'Well, just that it's not my usual manner to shoot at people — '

'You don't have to explain, ma'am. I think I understand, and you made the right choice in that instant when you saw me. I'm indebted to you.'

The hard lines and creased brow softened somewhat but she was still troubled. Benteen knew how difficult this must be for her and he wanted to put her mind at ease.

'I've made things difficult for myself with these men,' she said at last.

'Maybe not all of them. I've been thinking on this problem and the way I see it only a few of those hardcases will be any trouble.'

'How can you be so sure?'

'A cowboy puts his time in and collects his pay. Each day he relies on the routine of rounding up strays, riding fence, and taking care of the horses. It's hard work but the familiarity of it is what they want. Most of them couldn't care whether they carry a gun and wouldn't, if not for the rustlers or Indians.'

'I see. But I have no way of knowing how many are involved in this.'

'If that man upstairs survives I reckon in a few days he'll be able to tell us who did this. He had to see his attackers. They were shot at close range.'

'I see, yes, that does seem practical.'

Practical indeed. Benteen hadn't heard the word in years. His wife had liked things to be practical, as she often said, but then she was gone and nothing about Benteen's life had been practical. Now here was this woman, this perfect stranger, telling Benteen that he was being practical. And she was lovely. In the glow of the oil lamp her skin looked soft, her eyes shining. She was curious, and perhaps a little frightened, but Benteen admired her. She had made a choice and held her dignity intact. He had not looked at a woman this closely in a long time. He felt attracted to her, as any man would, but he also instinctively knew her interest in him wasn't romantic.

'Where are you from?' Rebecca asked. Her voice was but a whisper.

Benteen didn't want to talk about the past but he couldn't be rude. She deserved some kind of response. At length he said, 'After the war I had a ranch in Oklahoma but then my wife died.'

His voice sounded hollow and he knew his words left a lot of things unspoken.

'I'm sorry,' she said. 'You must have loved her very much.'

Benteen nodded. 'I've sort of been drifting ever since. I don't stay in one place for very long.'

They were silent a moment, each lost in their own thoughts. Then Rebecca said, 'I need to check on those girls. Elma has a soft touch but those youngsters will sleep better with two of us clucking over them.'

'This man Benson, do you know him well?'

'As well as I could. Dave and Josephine came into town about once a month for supplies. They usually came with the Nash family and the Talbots.'

'Other homesteaders?'

'Yes, their properties form a triangle out near the creek.'

'I didn't see any sign of them.'

35

'Gloria Nash lives with her brother. They're good people.' Her eyes misted up. 'I'd hate to learn something happened to them. It's such a horrible tragedy.'

Benteen nodded. 'I'll check on them tomorrow.'

'Thank you Mr Benteen.'

'Hank.'

'Hank,' she repeated, and with a tired smile she left him to his coffee.

Well, now I'm into it, he thought. *Sure as the sun comes up each morning the wind has pushed me into trouble. I'll make something good come of it if I can,* he vowed silently. *These are good people. I wouldn't mind it if I died with a gun in my hand, not if it can do some good.*

Then he pushed these thoughts aside and held his emotions firm while he sipped his coffee and allowed his body to relax. He would need his rest, after all. Later, Benteen made a pallet on the floor with his remaining blanket. He rested his head against his saddle and allowed his muscles to relax even further.

He tried to remain impassive, silent as stone, just as he had witnessed the Sioux on occasion when he was recovering from his injuries. The Sioux had a way of remaining calm even when he knew they were undergoing a stressful experience. Indians had learned long before the white man came to internalize their stress, to fold it up like a trinket they placed in their blankets, push it aside and wait. There was a time for fighting, just as there was a time for resting. But Benteen was a white man and the ways of the Sioux did not come easy to him. Still, he had learned to become passive and relax when under stress or when he was in danger, and this was a skill that few white men possessed.

He closed his eyes and in his mind he examined the faces of the men he had encountered. He studied each face, assessed its qualities, and made a judgment as to the character of the person whose image floated past his mind's eye. Walt Driggs. Mason Shrive. Those two could get him killed. Then he thought about Rebecca Deloney and he had to blink. He opened his eyes to his dim surroundings. Sleep was impossible for him. The best he could manage was this twilight state of relaxation. There was the faint rustle of activity in the quarters upstairs. He thought about Molly and Miranda and what they must be thinking. The two girls had not spoken one word to him. But when he found them he'd spoken to them in a low, soothing voice and they had obeyed his commands.

A coldness crept into his heart as he thought about the men who had killed Josephine Benson. Men? Somehow he sensed that more than one was involved. Benteen's instincts were never wrong. He was going to find out who it was and kill them. But how could he uncover the killers? Only by creating an event that set circumstances into motion would he get his answer.

Benteen could do that easily enough.

He had no intention of spending the entire night on Rebecca's kitchen floor, but there was no sense in telling her that. He wasn't the type of man who waited calmly when he knew trouble was coming. But he was the type of man who planned carefully and Benteen knew exactly what he would do next, and on that very night. What he didn't know was how many men he would have to kill.

3

'Hank Benteen!'

The name hung in the air and Shrive noted that Driggs had that odd look in his eyes again. Benteen was the topic of conversation amongst the cowboys, gunmen, drunks, drovers and whores who filled the saloon at ten o'clock that night. Shrive thought Driggs was about to have one of his spells. He looked at his fellow card-players and cursed under his breath. Driggs was deep into the whiskey, his calloused hands nervously stroking his beard or thumbing the edges of his cards. Joe Driscoll was the only one who hadn't said much, but then he didn't need to. He'd won every poker game they'd played that night, and it looked like he was about to win this one. The kid, Jake Nickles, had already proclaimed that he could beat Hank Benteen to the draw.

Ralph McCreedy, an old snaggle-toothed cowpuncher with a hot temper, chewed on the stump of a cigar. He was sweating profusely, his dark eyes watery, his skin jaundiced.

What an ungodly group they all made, Shrive thought. He wanted to be rid of them. Maybe this secret partnership he'd entered into with Walt Driggs had been a mistake. All of their carefully laid plans had gone to hell in a very short time, and now Hank Benteen had come riding into town with Dave Benson and his girls.

Of course Driggs had failed in that assignment, too. Now they faced a hangman's noose if Benson survived. Driggs had confronted Benson without him and botched it up. Without time to return and hide the bodies they'd been at risk, and then Benteen's arrival had been a stroke of bad luck. Benson would most certainly have died if not for Benteen. Shrive felt his stomach go sour. He held on to the slim chance that they could still eliminate Benson and Benteen both.

'No gunfighter is ever the fastest for long,' McCreedy said. 'Benteen ain't so special. I've drawn on men with a better reputation.'

'Go on!' exclaimed Jake. 'The way I see it I could probably outdraw him. He didn't look so high and mighty on that old horse. Hell, he looks like a tired old man who needs a bath.'

He chuckled and took a long draw from the whiskey bottle.

'You need to lay off that whiskey if you aim on gunning Benteen,' Shrive said.

The kid grunted. Driggs ran a filthy hand over his graying beard and said 'Goddamnit! I heard he was half Apache! If he's a half-breed then that gives us the right to shoot him on sight!'

At the bar a man named Kendrick watched them with interest. He was a tall man, dressed in black; Shrive knew Kendrick was a gunfighter. Boss Nickles had hired him just a few weeks earlier. Kendrick sipped a beer and smoked. Shrive had been keeping an eye on the man for thirty minutes. Something gnawed at Kendrick and it wouldn't be long before he said his piece.

Driggs was chattering nervously again, his hands in constant motion, his eyes flicking back and forth. 'If he killed ten men there's gotta be paper on him. There might be a reward. We could wire the marshal for confirmation and then string him up!'

'Oh hell!' Shrive said. 'He's one man. Even if he's fast with a gun there's too many of us. We need to stay calm and let Mr Nickles decide what to do.'

'But if Benson lives and talks — '

'Shut up, Driggs!' Shrive barked.

'I've got no time for a man who sides with sodbusters,' McCreedy said. 'I'm for shooting him on sight just because we can.'

'Why are you worried what Benson says?' Joe Driscoll asked.

'He's just blabbering,' Shrive cut in

sharply. 'You know Driggs here gets loco sometimes.'

Damn that Driggs for almost tipping their hand!

The whiskey had been flowing for several hours now and it showed in their faces like a map. They played cards furiously, not really caring who won or lost. The room stank of sweat and stale perfume. Occasionally one of the whores ambled to their table and tried to get some interest but tonight they had murder on their minds.

When a whore slid on to McCreedy's lap he squeezed her breast until it hurt. She squealed in pain. 'You don't have to be so rough!' she spat.

'Go away,' McCreedy said. 'I don't need a distraction before I kill a man.'

The pouting whore shuffled away and sought better prospects with a group of young cowboys who had just swung into the saloon.

Kendrick moved in their direction, wisely keeping his hands away from his gun.

'Benteen is fast,' he said. 'I saw him shoot a man in Cheyenne. The only way to take him is by surprising him.'

'You're Kendrick, right?'

The man nodded.

'And I suppose you know a way to surprise him?'

'No, as a matter of fact I don't. But pulling on him will only get you killed.'

'Why'd Boss Nickles hire you?' Shrive asked, although he already knew the answer.

'I came on to help with your sodbuster problem.'

'Well, I guess you came on a little late,' Driggs said harshly.

Kendrick chuckled and smiled. 'I get paid all the same. Mr Nickles doesn't want bloodshed, but if he's forced into it then I'm here to protect his interests.'

'Enough bullshit.' Jake said. 'My pa won't have to decide anything once I'm finished with Benteen.'

'What have you got against him?' Shrive asked.

'Nothin'. But he's a gunfighter and

he sides with those sodbusters. I don't need any more reason not to like him.'

Shrive thought it over and decided Jake Nickles might be a useful distraction. Benson had to be eliminated, and so did Benteen. Somehow he had to make it all work in his favor without anyone knowing.

Jake shuffled the cards and swigged from his whiskey bottle. *Young and stupid*, Shrive thought, the kid would get himself killed yet. That was certain, and the thought made him smile.

'Let's play cards!' Jake hooted, then with a malicious sneer he looked at Kendrick and said, 'Once I kill Benteen my pa can pay you off and you can ride out!'

Kendrick frowned and shrugged. But Shrive saw the look in his eyes and they both knew one thing for certain. With Kendrick and Benteen in town Pitchstone was about to heat up. Shrive wanted to make certain he didn't get caught in a crossfire.

★ ★ ★

Benteen waited patiently in the dark.
Near midnight he rose and stretched.
He needed his muscles loose before he
ventured into the street. He went to the
restaurant's window and peered out.
Lights blazed from the saloon. Like
almost everything in Pitchstone it
didn't have a name. The sign outside
simply stated SALOON just as Rebecca's sign read RESTAURANT. This
was a town in its infancy, poised on the
frontier and waiting to discover its
destiny.

Benteen knew that destiny would be
written in blood like that of so many
other towns that he had known. He felt
a vague sense of euphoria with the
knowledge of his coming actions. His
body was still hard and lean although
the years had begun to ask a price. He
looked on the street with a tranquil
fascination. A few lights burned in
some distant windows, but all of the
activity was centered on the saloon.

He normally kept his Colt loaded with five rounds, the hammer resting on an empty cylinder to prevent an accidental discharge should the gun be dropped. But tonight he strapped on his holster, pulled out the Colt and loaded a sixth cartridge into the empty cylinder. Then he loaded Dave Benson's Colt and stuck it in his belt. An extra gun might help.

He thought about Rebecca coming out of her restaurant with that Winchester. What a sight that had been! That gal had brass. Then he thought about the way she looked in the glow of the oil lamp, her hair catching the light, her soft, curving figure standing mere inches from him and that special glow in her eyes.

He brushed the thought aside. Years ago Benteen's wife had been killed by a stray bullet in a bank robbery. He'd spent a long year hunting the men responsible, and more years drifting. An Oglala Sioux medicine man had given him the name Wind Rider. He remembered the ancient creases around the man's eyes, the low timbre of his voice. The wind is the sky's strength, the old man had told him, and his destiny was written on the wind. With such a destiny he could not have a woman in his life until he found his shadow again. The trails he followed were long and treacherous, and one day the wind would push him toward his home.

Sometimes he thought the words of the old Indian were foolish, but deep down he knew it was all true. He'd been injured while hunting up in Montana and the old man had brought him to the Indian camp to heal. All that long winter he listened to the medicine man foretell his future . . .

He pushed aside the memories. A few moments later he slipped out of the restaurant and edged along the boardwalk. His finely tuned senses analyzed his dark surroundings. Satisfied that he was alone in the street he walked slowly toward the saloon. He stood motionless for a minute listening to the idle conversation.

Letting his right hand rest lightly on his holstered gun, he pushed through the batwing doors, raking his gaze around the room. His first thought was: *Too many tables*. The tables would be in his way. He instantly decided to hug the wall, and drifted right toward the bar where the grizzled barman eyed Benteen with suspicion.

The saloon was a combination of tidiness and filth. On one hand, some effort had been made to emulate the fancy saloons of places like Denver. An oil-painting of a curvaceous woman swathed in pink silk adorned the wall next to the bar. A full-length mirror also hung upon the wall, and the oil lamps were glittering in freshly cleaned funnel glass. But the floor was greased with grime and the spittoons looked not to have been cleaned in ages. The place needed a good sweeping.

The tables were crowded with men drinking and playing cards. A few of them had looked up when he entered but now they were all turning and staring at him. Conversation died to a whisper before silence hung like a pall over the room. The expressions on the hard, worn faces were either curious or outright contemptuous and more than a few of them recognized him. All of them were aware that his hand rested on his gun but none appeared concerned. Almost everyone in the saloon carried a gun.

Benteen took it all in, leaned against the bar at an angle so that he could watch the barman in his peripheral vision.

From upstairs came the sound of a hand smacking flesh and a whore squealed, but whether in pain or pleasure Benteen wasn't sure. A wry smiled crossed his lips.

He looked at each man at each table quickly but decisively and made an instantaneous judgment. The men who had confronted him earlier, Mason Shrive and Walt Driggs, sat at a table with a snaggle-toothed man, a middle-aged man and a young drover. Further back in the room four men appraised him intently. Two groups. The other men in the saloon were curious but none struck him as gunmen. It would be these two groups. Eight men.

'Bring me a beer,' he said to the barman.

Without saying a word the barman brought the beer. Benteen said, 'Now you stand down there and keep your hands on the bar.'

He looked at the crowd. They were ready, he knew, but how many would commit themselves was unknown. He decided to start the dance right then.

'My name is Hank Benteen,' he began. 'And I rode into town to help that wounded man, Dave Benson, and his two girls. I didn't come here looking for trouble. Helping folks in need is what all good people should do.'

They waited, watching. A fly buzzed into the saloon, drifting past with an irritating nonchalance.

'Dave Benson and his girls are under my protection, and that goes for the woman Rebecca Deloney. I'll kill any man who hurts them.'

Outside the night wind picked up and a wolf growled in a thicket.

The crowd murmured, a few nodded their heads understandingly.

The snaggle-toothed man with Shrive and Driggs said, 'You got some balls, coming in here and making threats.'

'It's not a threat,' Benteen said. 'I'm stating facts. Even an old drunk like you can understand that.'

'You don't seem too friendly,' a man at the far table said.

'I'm not friendly to those who kill women. Whoever killed the Benson woman is just a rabid dog. I shoot rabid dogs.'

Shrive and Driggs looked ready to draw. Anger turned their eyes into narrow slits, but there was hesitation in their faces, too. Especially in Driggs's. He had the look that Benteen had seen in men that had their spirits shattered

53

by the thunder of cannons and harrowing cries of the dying. He had seen such men long ago at a place called Shiloh. No, Driggs wouldn't draw. At least not today.

Shrive was a possibility but it was the kid, this young drover, who couldn't be more than eighteen. He would draw, and so would old Snaggle-Tooth, and those men at the table in the rear . . .

The snaggle-toothed man stood up and stepped away from his chair. Benteen didn't move.

'I heard about you. Some say you're faster than Wyatt Earp.'

'Earp isn't fast.' Benteen said. 'But he's accurate. Accuracy is everything in a gunfight.'

He could see that Snaggle-Tooth was thinking it through, trying to come up with a response.

'So what makes you so special?'

'I'm fast *and* accurate.' Benteen said calmly.

'Fast and accurate,' Snaggle-Tooth repeated, still thinking it through.

Snaggle-Tooth's fingers twitched and his shoulder dropped almost imperceptibly although Benteen noticed it. He was far too slow, his fingers still curling on the walnut stock of his gun when Benteen's Colt belched flame and smoke. The gunshot thundered in the room, the smell of gunsmoke instantly pervading the air.

The bullet took Snaggle-Tooth in the larynx and blew out his neck. A wave of blood burst from the exit wound as his body toppled and he thumped face down on the greasy floor, his legs twitching in their death spasm.

The saloon erupted with movement and noise: men dove for cover or scrambled to their feet, some colliding as they rushed to safety.

Benteen strode purposefully into the fray. Driggs had crawled under a table and Shrive threw up his hands. 'No!' he rasped, but the young drover clawed a Colt from his holster and Benteen slammed his Peacemaker's butt into the kid's nose, shattering it. The kid bellowed in pain and Benteen swept his arm across his face, his gunbutt slamming into the kid's head. As the kid went down the four surly men at the rear table had regained their composure and were pulling their guns.

A gun barked and a bullet whizzed past Benteen's head.

Benteen crouched, fired, scrambled to his left, rose up and fired again.

His first bullet slammed into a man's chest. His second bullet tore through another man's shoulder, exited with a spray of blood and bone before the slug thunked into the wall. Benteen fired again and the man took a second slug in his belly. He howled and crashed to the floor.

A man clad in black caught his eye. Benteen recognized the man as a hired gunmen from Cheyenne — John Kendrick — backing toward the door. Their eyes locked and Kendrick showed the palms of his hands. Kendrick was letting Benteen know he wasn't a part of it. In that instant another man rushed him. Big, smelling of sweat and booze, the man barreled toward Benteen and the Colt bucked in his hand, spewing lead. He was so close the blast ignited the man's shirt as the bullet tore a lethal path through his ribcage, smearing a bloody hole through his lungs and blowing out his spine. A grotesque mask of pain was etched across the man's face as he fell to the floor, his blood pumping out with each weakening heartbeat.

'Enough!' Shrive yelled. He rose from the floor, still holding his hands high. 'You made your point, now you can go. There's no need for all of this killing.'

The young drover whom Benteen had knocked out was groaning on the floor. One man in the rear remained standing. It was down to him, Shrive, the kid and Driggs who was huddled and shaking with fear under a table.

Benteen felt a twinge of sympathy for Driggs. During the war he had seen many men lose their nerve in battle, and many of them ended up like

Driggs, broken and shivering, their pants wet with their own urine. But he also knew that a wounded grizzly would still attack with its last breath. He would have to be wary of Driggs.

He turned his attention to the man in the rear while holding his Colt on Shrive. The man he considered a final threat was short, stocky, maybe thirty. He had the hard, worn edge of a cowpuncher.

'Tell me your name.' Benteen said.

'Joe Driscoll.'

'You going to try and gun me later?'

The man shook his head. 'I would have pulled on you if I was going to try. I reckon I'm out of it.'

Benteen looked at Shrive. 'You all work for Nickles?'

'We do, and there's gonna be questions he'll have for you.'

'Tell him he can ask his questions after he pays for a proper burial for these four men.'

Benteen lowered his Colt and stepped back to the bar. 'Tell Nickles what I said and that if he comes gunning for me he'll die first.'

The young drover pulled himself up, glared at Benteen. 'You son of a bitch!'

'Easy kid. I saved your life. Don't waste it now by pulling that hogleg.'

The kid spat a bloody wad of mucus on the floor. 'You broke my nose!'

'I reckon you should see a doctor.'

Shrive stepped in front of the kid.

'Easy, Jake. You can't beat him. There's gonna be another day.'

'You're damn right there will be!' The kid spat again.

Shrive frowned. He looked at Benteen and said, 'This is Jake Nickles. I guess not killing him was the smartest thing you've ever done, but his pa is gonna have questions.'

'He's gonna skin your hide!' Jake hissed.

Suddenly Benteen was very tired. He wondered if the years were catching up with him after all. Maybe it was that and the fact that these men bored him with their misguided anger, their false bravado and mean temperament. He had seen and killed too many men like them.

He holstered his Colt and lifted the beer that he'd ordered when he walked in. He downed the beer in two gulps, set the empty glass on the bar and wiped his mouth with his sleeve.

'Good beer,' he said. He fished a silver coin from his pocket and flipped it toward the bartender, who stood with mouth agape.

'You'll see us again,' Shrive said.

Benteen walked to the batwing doors, stopped, and turned to face the awestruck crowd. 'Maybe that's when I'll kill you,' he said. 'Or maybe I'll wait a bit.' He sighed and took a breath. They all continued staring at him but none was ready to move against him. Then he said, 'Just remember what I said and maybe you sons of bitches will live to be old men after all.'

He took a last look around. Too many angry eyes stared back at him, but he didn't see Kendrick again. No matter that Kendrick had taken his leave, the man's very presence in town might spell trouble. The last thing Benteen saw before he pushed through the batwing doors was Driggs under the table shaking and snarling like a wounded animal. Hell, the man was shellshocked, that much was obvious.

Benteen knew that Shrive or Kendrick might present a problem later, but right now Driggs was the one to watch.

4

At sunrise Benteen was at the crest of a hill a mile from the charred remains of the Benson ranch. One rider had followed him, possibly two, but had yet to make an antagonistic move. Benteen assumed it was John Kendrick. There was nothing to do but wait and see if the man meant him harm. Benteen was ready if he did.

In the pale morning light the landscape was stark, nearly barren of life. But Benteen noticed things that other men missed. From his vantage point he could see a wagon trail heading northeast and another heading southwest. The Bensons had chosen a place called the Gros Ventre Range near Bull Creek and Bear Creek. This was rugged but beautiful country in the shadow of the Bridger-Teton Mountains.

Rebecca had said that the Nashes and Talbots were the other homesteaders. Benteen wanted to talk with them to find out what he could about Charles Nickles and his cowhands. He rode northeast, careful to keep himself off the crest of any hills where his silhouette would make a nice target. He spurred his horse along the profusion of swales and valleys.

Presently he came to a plain where the land was in turmoil. It was a post hole that caught his eye first. A post hole but no fence. Benteen urged his horse along the invisible fence line and counted fourteen post holes. He pushed up from his saddle and squinted at the earth. Then he saw the charred remains of another cabin, the timbers blackened and jutting from the rubble like the remains of some prehistoric beast.

He had no doubt this had been one of the homestead ranches, but all that was left were these charred remains. A chill ran down his spine. He knew they were all dead although there wasn't a shred of evidence to suggest this. But Benteen knew.

He tugged his horse's bridle and made a clacking sound with his tongue. The horse obeyed and eased around in a circle as Benteen scrutinized the soil.

There were post holes and indentations in the earth and a few scraps of splintered wood; those signs alone told the tale. These fences had all been removed! Someone had wanted those fences down, and only a cattleman would feel that his interests were threatened by the homesteaders.

Benteen knew the Sioux could move a large village in a short time without leaving much sign of their presence, but the Sioux moved out of necessity. A fence line was meant to be permanent. The cabins had been burned and the fence lines removed. It was a clear signal. He knew it would be the same story when he went southwest toward the other cabin, but he had to see for himself. The sun was higher now and birds sang in the trees that bordered this small valley.

The wind brought him the sound of a lever rifle snatching up a cartridge and nestling it in the breech.

It was the wind that offered up the sound and his knowledge of firearms told him it was an 1866 Henry. The thought flashed through his mind in the same instant that he pulled the reins left and hunched his shoulders as the bullet buzzed harmlessly past just as the rifle shot shattered the morning's calm.

He dismounted, grabbed the reins and quickly led his horse into a gully. He followed a deer trail for half a mile and then left his horse nibbling at some grass while he clambered up a hill for a look. Benteen was calm. If it was Kendrick he might have some trouble because he knew Kendrick was good with a gun. Still, Benteen had the advantage of not caring whether he lived or died. He wouldn't go down easily; making the bastards work for his blood was a matter of personal honor. But if he died, well, so be it. This was a good day to die.

A group of pine trees along a ridgeline appeared to have been the shooter's position. That meant he was moving east and trying to circle around. It would be impossible for the shooter to get close as long as Benteen was vigilant. Both the shooter and Benteen knew this would be a cat-and-mouse game played out with rifles. So be it.

He returned to his horse and pulled a '73 Winchester from the saddle boot. Thumbing cartridges into the magazine he reversed direction, went up over a ridge and took up position near a clump of scrub and sage.

He waited twenty minutes, barely moving during that entire time. He breathed slowly. The sun was hot on his back but his wide-brimmed Stetson helped shade his eyes. Then he saw the other man leading his horse, followed by a second man. Two riders hunting him would make the game interesting, Benteen thought.

Neither man was Kendrick.

And they aren't too smart, thought Benteen.

Both men were walking their horses and doing nothing to protect themselves. They were either overconfident or damn fools. Benteen decided damn fools was more likely. After he killed them he expected to find gold coins in their pockets. Well-paid damn fools often died young.

They were 250 yards away, moving west to east. Benteen raised his rifle and set his sights on the larger of the two men. He let the muzzle's sight drop to the man's abdomen, took a breath, breathed out and squeezed the trigger. The Winchester boomed and several pheasants immediately took flight. The shot echoed across the sagebrush.

A shadow flew from the man's back as the bullet ripped through his belly. Benteen knew it was probably fatal. The man would bleed out in a few minutes. He watched him slump to the ground as his companion scrambled for cover.

The other man lifted his rifle and

sent a shot toward Benteen but the slug was wide, tearing up dirt twenty feet to Benteen's left.

Benteen held his rifle steady and swung left as the other man scrambled for cover. Benteen's Winchester cracked in the hot morning air and a puff went up from the man's boot. The slug had caught the man's left leg just above the ankle. He howled and went down.

Benteen lowered his rifle and began approaching the two men. He circled wide, coming in from the right, his rifle at port-of-arms.

A Colt barked twice as the second ambusher sent shots flying into a clump of sagebrush. From his position he couldn't see Benteen approaching his dying comrade. He was desperate, firing at dust.

The first man was slumped against a rock, his hands bloody from the wound on his belly. His face was contorted in agony.

'You done killed me,' he said as Benteen approached. 'You gotta promise me a decent burial.'

His yellow eyes rolled back into his head as he wheezed and coughed up a glob of blood.

'I'll see to it you get buried proper,' Benteen said, 'if you tell me who sent you after me.'

'Walt Driggs paid us . . . said you had a bounty on yer head. Paid us in gold, he . . .'

A tremor shook the man and his tongue snaked out, licking blood from his lips. Then he coughed up more blood and died.

Gold had turned to lethal lead for this man, Benteen thought. It always did.

He turned his attention to the second ambusher. He was a hundred yards away, down the incline of a small hill. Benteen circled again, hoping to come at the man from behind. He levered a round into the Winchester, crouched and moved into position. When he was ten feet from the crest of the hill a gray-haired head bobbed up followed by a hand holding a Colt. The gun spat lead that plunked into the dirt near Benteen's boot.

Benteen dove, fired, and rolled. Then he straightened and ran in a wider circle still looking for any advantage the rolling plain might offer.

The ambusher fired twice more. Wild shots that tore at blue sky and dust.

Five shots. Had the man loaded six? Most cowpunchers kept the hammer down on an empty cylinder for safety. Only gunmen and bounty hunters loaded six before a gunfight. These men had obviously been hired in a saloon. Rank amateurs sent to do a killer's job. Benteen held himself in check and breathed slowly. Then he heard the tell-tale sound of the Colt's cylinder spinning. The familiar *snick-clack* meant he was loading.

He sprang to his feet and ran. When he crested the hill the man was plugging his last bullet into the Colt. He thumbed the loading gate closed, cocked the hammer and would have shot Benteen had it not been for the

Winchester's slug tearing a hole through his forehead. The man's final, desperate thought was splattered across the sage and dry grass.

Benteen turned his eyes away from the corpse, still half-expecting Kendrick or Driggs to spring another ambush. But the wind picked up and with it came the scent of wild blooming flowers mingled with the morning songs of birds.

His morning ride had brought him answers but questions still lingered. What role was Kendrick playing in all of this? Where were the bodies of the Nash and Talbot families? Benteen would get answers soon enough, but for now he had to be satisfied with one thing — a dying man had implicated Walt Driggs in the ambush. That meant Driggs was fair game.

Benteen reloaded his Winchester. Then he set to tying the dead men to their horses. It was time to head back to Pitchstone.

5

Three days passed without incident. During that time the town buzzed with talk about Benteen. He'd killed two more men and demanded again that Charles Nickles pay the funeral costs. Riders set out for the Nickles ranch. Word spread that Nickles himself was coming to square things with Benteen. Speculation was rampant that each man would kill the other in a gunfight. Some placed bets that Benteen would survive, others bet on Nickles. Benteen took note of the fact that Walt Driggs had gone missing. He made a few inquiries and the general feeling was good riddance. Driggs worked for Nickles but that didn't make him popular.

On the third day Dave Benson was well enough to talk. Benteen was anxious to hear what the man had to say. But he spent a good hour with his daughters as Rebecca fussed over him. The girls were thrilled to see their father sitting up in bed and talking. They cooed around him, two vibrant but gentle girls who, Benson said, possessed the best qualities of their mother. The man's grief was evident on his face and Benteen took his leave.

He drank coffee in the restaurant as Elma handled the waitressing chores. The old woman was loyal to Rebecca but made poor company. Elma was a sourpuss from her laced-up shoes to the top of her faded bonnet. Once, when Benteen was helping himself to a slice of beef in the kitchen, she shuffled over to him and said, 'See to it that you keep your thoughts pure when you're around Miss Deloney. She's too young for you. A woman like her can find a decent man to marry, and it'll happen yet. You just wait and see.' With that Elma turned her back on him and left the room.

Her remark stung Benteen. At fifty-two he had come to the realization that his life was ebbing, as all lives must. But Rebecca had kindled long-dormant feelings in him. He had to admit the thought had crossed his mind that he could settle down. He had done it once. But Mary was dead these many years and now he was a Wind Rider.

An image flashed through his mind of the Sioux medicine man, his leathery face ablaze with firelight as he smoked his pipe in the tepee, those cold winter nights long ago. He looked up. Rebecca had entered the room with the two girls. 'Dave wants to see you,' Rebecca said. 'The girls here and I are going to make lunch and then I'm going to teach them about running a restaurant.'

Benteen took it that her practical, businesslike manner was assumed partly to benefit the girls. But he saw in her eyes that she would want to know every-thing Dave Benson said to him. And looking at her standing there he knew he'd tell her.

Benson was sitting in a chair near the window drinking coffee. He was pale and gaunt but his eyes danced with the knowledge that he would live.

'I'm obliged to you,' Benson said.

'I wish I could have done more.'

'Walt Driggs killed my wife. He'd been coming around trying to buy the ranch. I refused and then he began making threats. He said he'd run us off.' Benson paused. 'When I'm well enough I'm going to gun him.'

Benteen nodded. He pulled a Colt from his belt and handed it to Benson. 'I cleaned your gun. It's loaded. Keep it near you from here on. Your Sharps is downstairs in the kitchen.'

'You know Driggs?'

'Seen him around town. Sometimes he's with a fellow named Mason Shrive. Driggs went missing a few days ago.'

Benteen told Benson everything that had occurred while he was on the mend.

'Driggs is loco,' Benson said. 'Everybody knows it although nobody can say exactly what's wrong with him. He's either ridden on or he's hiding, waiting to make a play.'

'You think Nickles or his no-good son were in on this?'

'I don't know. The way I see it they wanted that land. We had the legal right to it. We all filed claims. You say there's no sign of the others? The Talbots and the Nash family? No sign at all?'

'I fear the worst. Somebody wants that land cleared. It had to be a huge effort to remove those fence lines so cleanly. It would take strong-willed men with a wagon. It's the damndest thing I've ever seen.'

'Nickles has to be a part of it. Nothing else makes sense.'

'We'll know soon enough. He's on his way here. Dave, I know it's difficult but you have to tell me more about what happened. Was Mason Shrive with Driggs?'

'No, I only saw Driggs. We were having our afternoon lunch when he rode up. I hid the girls right away. Driggs had been making threats that he would run us off. He called out to us and Josephine and I . . . ' Benson stopped, his features tight and flushed. His lip was trembling and Benteen looked away a moment. After some moments Benson composed himself and continued:

'Josephine and I armed ourselves. She walked out ahead of me before I could stop her.' Again Benson paused. 'She was cut down instantly and then I remember firing the gun.' A sad, faraway look crept into the man's eyes.

'There were horse-prints all over that place,' Benteen said. 'But I think he was alone.'

'He wanted the deed to my land.' Benson said. 'He said he'd even buy it from me, but his offer was less than half the value. I laughed in his face. If somebody put him up to it I'll get the names of the others when I hunt him down.' Benson leveled his stare at Benteen. 'Now you listen to me. Driggs is mine. I'm going to kill him. Nobody is to touch him but me.'

Benteen nodded. 'Unless he tries to

gun me. You still have a long road ahead. Be a few months before you're solid again.'

'We don't have that much time. A few weeks at the most. If they killed the Nash and Talbot families then . . . ' Benson's voice trailed off. What he was saying was undoubtedly true, and once word got out that two families had been murdered the territory would become a battlefield.

'What we need is proof,' Benson said. 'They had to bury those bodies somewhere.'

'It would be a gamble to find those graves.' Benteen thought it over a moment. 'The best I could do is ride a wide circle and look for signs.'

'If Nickles is coming to town he'll have plenty of men with him. You don't want to get caught alone out there.'

Benteen's mouth curled into a thin smile. 'We'll see. The thing now is for you to sit tight and heal. I'll have Rebecca bring up that Sharps. She has that Winchester down in the kitchen, too, and she's not afraid to use it.'

Benteen left Benson to rest and went out of the restaurant. Rebecca was helping Elma with the lunch crowd. She gave him a questioning glance as he passed but Benteen kept his gaze steady. He would talk with Rebecca later. For now he had to get a feel for things. He always functioned best when he had time to think things through.

He plopped himself in a chair outside the saloon and pulled out his tobacco pouch. He rolled himself a thin cigarette and smoked quietly while he stared at the dusty street. A few passersby took note of him but left him alone. The townspeople were now accustomed to his presence but gave him a wide berth. Benteen knew the best way to learn things was to listen. About half the townies were sympathetic to the cattlemen, but the rest were noncommittal. One fact stood out — most Westerners followed their own code of honor. It wasn't something that was written down, Benteen knew, but it was just as real and important as any document. No matter whether they agreed with the homesteaders or the cattleman, murder wouldn't be tolerated. Especially the murders of women and children. Josephine Benson's killing had already inflamed tempers. And several of the townies treated Benteen with a begrudging respect because he had saved Dave and his two little girls.

Benteen decided the only way to handle Charles Nickles was straight on, just like roping a bull. There was no fancy way about it. Benteen would either be killed on the spot or be allowed to have his say.

The afternoon waned, but he didn't have long to wait. He spied the dust in the sky twenty minutes before they rode in. That much dust meant he had brought plenty of men. Benteen wondered if his reputation as a gunman had given Nickles pause? Had the rancher brought that many men to protect himself? He supposed it didn't matter.

Charles Nickles rode his palomino at

the forefront of a group of twelve men. Even from a distance Benteen could see that Nickles was an imposing man. Tall, with a handlebar mustache streaked with gray, hazel eyes that shone with ferocity under the brim of his black Stetson. His clothing was immaculate; new snakeskin boots and silver spurs that clanged like music; clean riding-pants and a vest with gold buttons. The chain of a pocket watch dangled from his vest pocket. This was a man with money, and a man who took pride in his appearance.

Mason Shrive rode next to him, behind came John Kendrick, Joe Driscoll, the cowboy who had decided wisely against pulling a gun on Benteen. And Jake Nickles, his nose still bandaged, rode on the other side of his father. The older men all looked to be capable gunmen. Shrive saw Benteen and said, 'That's him.'

Nickles rode up to the saloon and stared down at Benteen, who hadn't moved from his chair.

'Are you Hank Benteen?' His voice was powerful, commanding.

'I am.'

'You broke my son's nose. You killed Ralph McCreedy and five other men who worked for me. Are these facts true?'

'I never asked the names of the men I killed. Four in the saloon and two outside of town. They all attacked me first. You've men riding next to you who will attest to those facts.'

'We don't know what happened to the men he killed outside of town. He might have bushwhacked them!' Jake said angrily. 'He's a gunman and a liar!'

Now Benteen stood up. Tension hung in the air. In his peripheral vision Benteen saw Rebecca outside her restaurant, the Winchester in her hand. The street had filled with people. Damn near the entire town had come out to witness this showdown. Whatever happened next there would be plenty of witnesses. He kept his right hand away from his gun and looked Jake Nickles in the eye.

'That's not a friendly thing to say. That type of talk can get a man killed. I spared your life once. See to it that you understand me because sometimes once is all you get.'

Jake went pale.

'By God, mister, you have a lot of brass!' Charles Nickles roared. 'I'm sitting here with a dozen armed men at my side. One word from me and you're a dead man! Now give me one reason why I shouldn't kill you right this instant!'

Benteen exhaled cigarette smoke and held a steady gaze eye to eye with Nickles. 'Dave Benson told me earlier today that Walt Driggs killed his wife. He rides for you, doesn't he? And then there's the matter of the Nash and Talbot families. They're missing and their ranches have been burned out.'

A murmur swept through the crowd. Benteen glanced at Shrive and saw a sheen of perspiration on his face. Jake

Nickles looked downright confused.

'What the hell do you mean, their ranches are burned?' Now Nickles was speaking in a softer tone. The gravity of the situation hadn't been lost on him.

'There's nothing left but burned timbers,' Benteen continued. 'Someone who doesn't agree with the Homestead Act has decided to take matters into their own hands. I believe those families were murdered and I think it's obvious Walt Driggs is behind it. The question is, who else? Driggs rides for you. You have the men, money and influence.' Nickles had turned red, his eyes blazing with open scorn at Benteen, but he remained silent.

'Now what I'm saying is simple.' Benteen glanced around at the crowd of people, many of whom had moved closer to hear better. 'Everybody in town has heard this and now the story is out. I believe the law says a man is innocent until proven guilty. Right now Walt Driggs is the only one implicated. But there's a weight on your shoulders now and I'm not the one who put it there. You can shoot me down but the story will get out, and eventually a marshal will ride into town looking for answers.'

Benteen let his right hand drop to his side, wavering near his gun. His intent was clear. He would kill as many as possible before they cut him down.

Nickles appeared to grow larger in his saddle as he took a breath. Slowly he dismounted and just as slowly he strode toward Benteen. And Benteen, ever vigilant and unafraid, never flinched as Nickles stood before him, his entire being exuding strength and power. Those watching would not soon forget the sight, for Benteen stood his ground well and there on the boardwalk an impasse was reached as each man appraised the other, each refusing to back down, each refusing to go for his gun.

Tension and silence stretched into an eternity.

A horse nickered.

A slight breeze came up the street

and gently touched both men.

Had Benteen smiled? At that moment Nickles exhaled and said, 'Harrumpf! Have a drink with me.' Then turning briefly toward his men he barked, 'You men find another place to drink. But no gunplay. The man that pulls his gun this day answers to me.' With that he strode purposefully into the saloon, his silver spurs jangling like a song.

The bartender, who had been listening and watching this unfold near the window, suddenly found himself serving whiskey to two men who frightened him to death. Sensing this, Nickles said, 'Relax, Burt. I won't shoot you unless you don't pour us a drink right quick!'

With whiskey in hand Benteen and Nickles appraised each other once more. Nickles was first to speak.

'My son's none too smart but he's not bad. He's not in on this. I'll kill Driggs myself if we find him. And by the way, I'm not part of it either. I'm an honest man, Benteen, but I don't take kindly to people implying otherwise.'

'Just so you understand the position we're both in.'

'I understand it.' He sipped his whiskey. 'You're right, Driggs had to have help. He's not smart enough to think of all this by himself.'

'That's about the way I figured it. What about Shrive? He's friendly with Driggs.'

'Could be. I can have the man watched. He hasn't been with me much longer than Driggs. Some of these men come and go every few years.'

Benteen nodded. He was a drifter himself so everything Nickles said had the ring of truth. 'You've got Kendrick out there. Why's he here?'

A long silence ensued while Nickles weighed his response carefully.

'Those sodbusters made threats,' He said at last, his voice low. 'Benson most of all. He's got backbone. I didn't want my men involved in any gunplay. I hired Kendrick for muscle. If it came to gunplay he could solve it and ride on. Those sodbusters are tough but no match against Kendrick. It seemed like a simple solution.'

'But they probably thought you hired him to kill them.'

'It was a mistake. Kendrick has instructions not to shoot unless fired on. I never thought things would get out of hand.'

Benteen judged from the tone of his voice that Nickles was telling the truth. He was relieved, but that also changed everything. He realized that none of them had any clue as to who had helped Driggs.

'I can't fight the Homestead Act,' Nickles said. 'But I can negotiate with them. I was prepared to offer those sodbusters a deal. I would be willing to pay a fee to allow my cattle to range on their property. That's fair. The money would help them and I could keep my cattle grazing.'

'But now those families are missing. I need to look around, see if I can find proof. Otherwise the law will only assume they packed up of their own will.'

'That's grim work,' Nickles said. 'You know Kendrick?'

'We've met.'

'I'll send him along. Two guns and two sets of eyes are better than one.'

'I work alone.'

'Then I'll ask it as a favor. Ride with Kendrick. We don't know how many men we're up against here.'

Benteen had to admit the man's plea was square.

'All right. And Benson will be left alone?'

'You have my word. You need money?'

Again Benteen nearly smiled. It was an almost imperceptible tugging at the corners of his mouth.

'Don't need any. But thanks for the offer.'

Nickles was surprised but didn't argue.

'You were down in Cheyenne last year. I heard you had a gunfight down there?'

'A foolish drunk thought he was as fast as Wild Bill.'

'Alcohol and guns have been the death of many men.'

'How many herd of cattle do you have?' Benteen wanted to change the subject.

'Seven thousand. I have eighty men working for me. It's thirty years since I came to this territory.'

'That sounds like a fine spread.'

'Hard work is what it is. But more homesteaders are coming into the area. There's going to be trouble in Johnson County. I don't want that kind of trouble here, but I'll fight if I have to. But this group is small. There's no reason for bloodshed.'

'Dave Benson might be a hard man, and he's lost his wife. Maybe you should talk to him.'

Nickles thought this over. 'I will at that. I'll not have people calling me a woman-killer. There might be a way we can settle this all fairly. I'll talk to Benson.'

With that Nickles finished his drink and set the glass on the bar. Then the two men shook hands and parted.

6

Walt Driggs remembered the first one when he was fifteen years old. Her name was Amanda Driggs and she was his mother. She hated the sight of him. She hated him because he was the bastard son that got in the way.

It was a month after his fifteenth birthday when she came home drunk with one of her men. Driggs had spent the day doing his chores on their small farm in the Texas panhandle when he heard the buggy rattle in the distance. She'd been gone a week and in all that time Driggs never let up on his chores. The farm kept him busy. They had cows, pigs and chickens, and a small garden to tend. He kept busy but his mind always wandered, turning over and examining the things he wanted. The way he saw the men turn a silver coin between their thumb and forefinger, taunting his mother with it until they eventually relinquished the coins in exchange for a few moments in her bedroom. As he grew older it excited him and he wanted to be a part of it.

That day Amanda came into the house and sat at the table. The man this time was tall, but older than usual with gray wisps at his temples. He had a beard stubble and his eyes were watery and bloodshot. They were both drunk.

'Get us some supper,' his mother said. She was tall also, and attractive without making the effort. Her dark hair was out of place but it gave her a vibrancy. Driggs liked the way his mother looked when she was drinking. Her features took on a glow; her eyes shone and her cheeks were red as if she had come in from the cold.

'I haven't had time to make anything.'

His mother looked at him. 'Why not? What you been doin' all day?'

When she spoke his heart beat faster

with anticipation. There was nothing he could do to please her. Dinner wasn't ready and it added to her contempt for him. His mother got up from the table and hit him. He never tried to stop her. She hit him with the flat of her hand across his cheek and the sting was like a dozen needles piercing his flesh.

'Yer good for nothin'.'

Without another word she pulled the man up from the table and led him into her bedroom. She didn't bother to shut the door. Driggs had reeled back from the blow and was leaning against the table, savoring his arousal. But today it was too hard to control.

Driggs went to the mantel and pulled the Sharps down from the pegs. Loading the rifle, he stood by the bedroom door and watched as the older man writhed with his mother. He shot the man in the back of the head, just as he was grunting with particular pleasure.

His mother screamed.

Driggs stared at her. He stared at the

splash of blood across her face, across the pillow. Her eyes shrank in her head and became small dark stones. A tremor ran through her body. She struggled to push the bleached lifeless body away from her.

'You bastard!'

The words spit like venom.

Driggs set the rifle down and grabbed the dead man's ankle. He pulled hard and the body slid to the floor with a thump. When his mother tried to cover herself with a sheet Driggs ripped it from her hands. He leaned in close to her, enjoying the warm, bristling sensation of her flesh. When she tried to get free he hit her so hard his knuckles stung. Later, when he was finished with her, Driggs placed his calloused hands around her neck and strangled her. Not long after he was down in Alabama with the Confederate forces.

Now he found himself on the run. Shrive had set this up but Shrive didn't understand the pleasure Driggs took from killing.

He enjoyed it!

Shrive had come up with the plan to kill the sodbusters and take their land. Once the sodbusters were out of the way they could sell those parcels to Mr Nickles. But Benteen had ruined all of that. Ruined the fun he'd had with those sodbusters, ruined the fun he might have in the future.

But Benteen scared him, too. Driggs felt ashamed by this weakness. It was something he couldn't control. After the war there were moments when the fear gripped him like cold metal and he was paralyzed with fright.

He had to stop Benteen. Shrive told him what happened, the way Benteen and Nickles faced off against each other only to part friends. Shrive was nervous and decided to lie low. Everything they had worked for was in jeopardy, and if Benteen succeeded in finding those bodies . . .

Driggs couldn't stand it. He was close to losing all of those erotic pleasures he derived from killing. Oh, no, that wouldn't do at all. He had to stop Benteen, but Driggs wasn't a gunman. He would have to ambush him.

But how? Where?

Shrive said Benteen was looking for the bodies. If he looked long enough he was certain to find them. Driggs let the plan take shape in his mind as he spurred his horse into the foothills. He had to assume that a capable man like Benteen would find those bodies after a time. That was where Driggs planned his ambush. He would kill Benteen and Kendrick at the gravesite. He had a rifle and he was a good shot. All he had to do now was kill Benteen and that damn fool Kendrick.

Driggs snapped his reins and spurred his horse into a gallop.

He would have his pleasure after all.

* * *

Benteen told Rebecca he would be gone a few days. He filled her in on his meeting with Nickles. When he was finished she gently placed her hand on his shoulder and said, 'Hank, please be careful.' He felt a warm tingling spread through him but quickly brushed the emotion aside. She gave him some freshly baked biscuits for his saddle-bag.

Rebecca was relieved that Nickles had given his word that Benson was safe from harm, but Benteen told her to keep her rifle handy just in case. Rebecca agreed. He left her on the boardwalk. He brought his horse around and pulled himself into the saddle. When he looked at her the early afternoon sun was tangled in her hair and her skin seemed to glow, soft and velvety; suddenly everything in life that Benteen had missed welled to the surface and he was forced to look away. He felt old, older than his years.

Kendrick was waiting down the street.

'Just so we understand each other,' Benteen said, 'I'm in charge and you're along as a favor I'm doing for Nickles.'

'All right, you're the foreman. Since we don't have a quarrel with each other let's keep it that way.'

Benteen nodded.

They took their time, moving slowly under the hot sun, enjoying the leisurely ride. The sky was an unending plain of blue and the sun was warm on their backs. Benteen paused at a bend in the river, Kendrick beside him, and they listened to the sound of water rushing over rocks. It was a clear, restful sound and Benteen thought he might come here one day soon and fish. There would be good trout and he would cook them over a fire on the grassy slope.

He made an affectionate clicking sound with his mouth and edged his horse across the river. He was sweating profusely now but the cold rushing water felt good on his legs. When they reached the other bank they stopped and he wiped the sweat from the band in his Stetson. To his right he spotted a small animal trail cutting through the underbrush and they followed that as he began to move south. He wanted to follow the river south and turn north where the foothills were thick with trees.

It was on days like this that he missed Mary the most. When she was alive they sometimes rode out together on fresh spring days and made a picnic along the riverbank. Her death fifteen years ago had come as a shock. No man should have his wife taken from him, and from that day on Benteen had begun to feel like an old man. He didn't like that feeling. He was fifty-two but he felt much older. Rebecca reminded him of Mary in small ways, but he had to shove those thoughts aside.

Sometimes he dreamed about Mary, and his dreams disturbed him. He was with Hancock's troops again near Hatcher's Run. They were under heavy artillery fire from batteries posted near Burgess's Tavern. The man next to him went down beneath a red halo as a rebel shell took away the side of his face. Then he would see Mary, dressed in a long white gown, floating above the gunsmoke, arms outstretched and beckoning to him.

Again pushing his intruding memories aside, Benteen pressed the roan into some thick underbrush, passing a cluster of rocks and a small spring. He examined the earth carefully and found no sign of riders. But it was just a matter of time, he knew, and he would eventually cut their trail.

They were methodical in their search, skirting the river, intent on fording a sign of riders. The afternoon shadows began to stretch when they circled into the foothills. Benteen was grateful that Kendrick wasn't the talkative sort. It was all about the money for him. He was doing a job, that was all.

At four o'clock that afternoon they cut across an old trail. The earth was marked by the deep imprint of iron-shod hoofs.

'Don't you think it's impossible for us to find any remains?' Kendrick said. 'This is a big country. They could be anywhere. We could ride past those graves and never know it.'

'There's always a sign,' Benteen replied. 'Something that tells a man passed this way.'

'I heard you got Indian blood. You plan on tracking them with Indian magic?'

'I'm no Indian,' Benteen responded. 'But I've spent time with the Sioux. I learned a great deal from them.' He pointed to the ground. 'You see these hoofprints? This is too far from any of the homesteader's property so it might be them. But the trail crosses that rocky plain. So we'll go up and take a look-see. A better view might help.'

Kendrick grunted.

They followed a switchback and an hour later they dismounted, leaving the horses to drink from a trickle of water that snaked down from the high rocks.

Kendrick pointed and said, 'Rider following us.'

Benteen saw the distant figure but couldn't make out the features. 'Mighty interesting,' Benteen said. 'We've got someone on our back trail and smoke in those trees.'

Now Kendrick followed Benteen's gaze and there it was, a tendril of smoke just at the treeline.

'That rider won't be able to see that smoke from down there. How do you want to play this, boss?'

Benteen caught the gentle jibe in Kendrick's tone. 'We'll ride to the smoke. We can stay out of sight by hugging the treeline. By the time we get near that camp it'll be dark.'

And so they did, swiftly, senses alert, fully aware that they were taking a risk by allowing the rider to advance without watching him, and although Kendrick wouldn't admit it, he agreed the smoke needed investigating. Besides, they'd expected to be followed. An hour later, with the sky turning the color of wine, they were close to the place where Benteen had seen the smoke.

They paused. Benteen leaned forward over the saddle pommel and listened to the forest sounds as the sun smoldered at the horizon. There was something: a sound he couldn't identify. He was absolutely still, shifting his weight slightly as his horse bent to nibble at some grass. He concentrated on the groves of pine that swept across the horizon before the purple shade of the mountains. He waited patiently, letting his peripheral vision sweep the treeline. He moved the horse up to a slight rise in the trail. There was the sway of branches in the breeze and a bird call. He saw a hawk circle briefly and dip below the cottonwoods. Then he saw a movement in the air, something like a ghost wavering at the tip of a cluster of tall pine.

Someone was down in that little hollow, with a campfire's smoke filtering up through the branches. It was barely perceptible, but Benteen had seen it. Leaving their horses tied to a branch in a deadfall, Benteen and

Kendrick worked their way slowly downhill through the tall pines. When they thought they were close they crawled through the underbrush, making their way down the slope tree by tree until they could hear voices. They were out of breath from their exertions, but they were careful not to make any sound. One dislodged rock or cracked branch would alert their quarry to their presence.

Benteen eased his way carefully through the brush, then wedged himself into a deadfall. He could hear pieces of conversation as he pushed with his elbows through the thicket.

' . . . don't drink too fast. You'll get sick.'

A weak voice answered. Benteen peered through the foliage at the camp. A woman sat near the fire. She was dressed in a man's clothing and was helping an injured man drink from a tin mug of coffee. There was a solitary horse tethered nearby.

'You lie back now. Night's coming

and you can sleep. Nothing can hurt us now.'

She was middle-aged, maybe Benteen's age or a few years younger, but still beautiful. Her red hair caught the firelight and shimmered. But her eyes were haunted, sad. Still, her beauty was something to ponder, even under these unusual circumstances. Both Kendrick and Benteen were astounded. Finding a woman and an injured man in this wild country, with the territory on edge because of the murders, was something akin to impossible. They looked upon the scene with amazement.

They retreated, carefully backing away until they were out of earshot.

'We need to offer to help,' Benteen said quickly. 'But we can't do it now. That woman has a Winchester nearby and she's wearing a gun in her holster. Night visitors in this territory can get killed right quick.'

'We should just ride on. It's none of our affair.' Kendrick's tone revealed his agitation.

'No, we won't.' Benteen was firm. 'In the morning we'll call out, identify ourselves and offer to help. That man looks to be in a bad way. I'll not turn my back on someone in need of help.'

'I don't like it,' Kendrick said, 'I'm getting paid by Nickles to do as he asks, and helping strangers wasn't part of the deal.'

All the same, Kendrick unsaddled their horses and led them to a small grove where they could nibble at the grass. They made camp and ate a meal of dried beef and some biscuits. Both men were silent, lost in their own thoughts. Once, just before the velvet sky slipped into its black cavern and plunged the world into night, Kendrick felt a slight breeze pick up. He glanced at Benteen and in that brief instant, with a soft night breeze whispering through the pines, he was startled to see a faraway look in Benteen's eyes, his face a mask of unbearable sadness.

7

Jake Nickles had a mission. He would kill Hank Benteen. It was the only way he could redeem himself. At long last, after years of self-doubt and uncertainty, he would prove to his father what kind of man he really was. And that was all of it, really. Prove to the old bastard he had some brass, too.

He rode along Benteen's back-trail, a sense of urgency spurring him on. His nose ached terribly. He had removed the bandage and the swollen skin itched as he rode headlong into the wind.

Twenty-one years of his father's discipline had taken its toll. He could drink and play cards and screw like a man, and now he would prove he could handle a gun. Tears welled in his eyes as he recalled the sight of Benteen entering the saloon. He remembered how he had felt as Benteen appraised

107

him with that ruthless gaze.

Fear! Pure and unfettered fear had swept through him. In that instant he realized he was no match for Benteen, but he had boasted in front of the men that he was fast on the draw. That was the liquor talking, but it was too late to back down. Once again the sound of Benteen's gun echoed in his mind; the sight of that Colt spewing flame and lead and old snaggle-toothed McCreedy falling dead on the floor. That horrifying moment was etched forever in his memory.

Their trail was easy to follow, which surprised him. Benteen and Kendrick were doing nothing to avoid pursuit. It was almost as if they welcomed an open attack. Such a brazen move, Jake knew, stemmed from their confidence — confidence that he had been lacking all of his life.

Hurtful, long-repressed feelings from his childhood welled to the surface. He blinked away tears. Always his father, the mighty Charles Nickles, had been a tough disciplinarian. When other children were playing after school Jake was sent to watch the men brand cattle or mend fences or round up strays. Then there were the menial but necessary chores — getting the chuckwagon ready for a trail drive, feeding the horses and replacing lost horseshoes. 'Learn how to handle horses,' his father had demanded, 'It's your lifeline on the trail.' So he learned about horses and cattle and fences, and he never had time to play. Never.

But now that was changed. Jake played like a man; he gambled and he drank. He spent time with whores and learned the way of flesh. But through it all his father never acknowledged him as a man, never showed him affection.

The Nickles breed were tough, unemotional men, and killers when they had to be.

Killing Benteen would do it. Killing Benteen would be a chance to hear his father say two simple words — well done. That was all he wanted. If he could just hear those words once he could just be himself. Just once. Well done.

He gritted his teeth. *Damn the old man to hell!*

He might have to backshoot Benteen and Kendrick. But then he could lie and claim they ambushed him and that he'd fired on them as they retreated. That would explain the bullet holes in their backs. Who would doubt his word?

Jake gnashed his teeth. Despair swept over him then, in great crashing waves, and reined his horse to a halt. What the hell had he gotten himself into? This wasn't what he wanted, but he had set out on his task and now he had to finish it.

The image of McCreedy's cold, dead eyes staring at the ceiling flashed through his mind. He was about to end up as dead as old snaggle-toothed McCreedy, and the entirety of his life would amount to nothing.

He looked out across the rolling hills and marked the way the sunlight changed every few moments. The mountains could be ruthlessly beautiful. He suddenly wanted to be home, back in the bunkhouse with the men, playing cards or just talking about the women they'd known. He didn't want to be here, stalled on the trail, waiting to attack a man who would kill him in an instant if he had the chance.

Then he remembered Walt Driggs. Somehow Driggs was behind the killings, and probably Mason Shrive was with him. What had spurred them into such a violent act? He was dismayed by his lack of knowledge. He knew something was going on — he'd overheard a few hushed words between the two men, but he hadn't given it much attention.

If he could prove that Driggs and Shrive were behind the attack against the Benson family his father might take notice. He would certainly take action against them. Another wave of despair crashed over him. He had nothing to go on. Only a hunch, and hunches like that meant nothing. His father was a tough but honorable man who would need proof against Driggs and Shrive before he would act.

Then he realized that if he killed Benteen he was destroying the only hope any of them had of discovering the truth. He knew why his father had sent Benteen and Kendrick out looking for Driggs; maybe if he offered to help Benteen he could somehow save face. And Benteen knew nothing of Shrive. All they had so far was Benson's word that Driggs had killed his wife, but Jake felt that Shrive was somehow involved.

He had to talk with Benteen.

For the first time in days a ray of hope appeared before him.

A sense of relief flooded his mind as he made a nickering sound and tugged the reins. His horse obeyed and started trotting again. If he could find Benteen now and convince him he meant no harm, together they might solve this murderous problem and bring peace to the valley. What would his father think of him then?

He gave his horse the spurs and set him into a steady gait. A soft wind brushed against him and he nearly smiled at the feeling. He wasn't accustomed to feeling good, and he wanted to feel good all the time. Now he had a start at something.

He'd heard what the men had said about Benteen. He had a mysterious past and the Indians had a name for him, Wind Rider. They made him out to be a mystical figure. Fast on the draw. A born killer. Now he had to find Benteen and rather than kill him, he had to convince Benteen that they were on the same side. Jake had no idea how he would do that.

It was getting dark. He would have to make camp for the night. The thought didn't please him. Benteen, Kendrick and Driggs were all out here doing the same. They would hunker down for the night, and each of them would kill Jake in an instant if they felt threatened.

Come morning, Jake would need a lot of luck just to survive till noon.

★ ★ ★

They called out to the woman in the morning. As expected, she was none too pleased to find two armed strangers approaching.

'My name's Hank Benteen and this is John Kendrick. We'll drop our guns. There's no reason for shooting, ma'am.'

'That's up to you. Just keep your hands where I can see them.'

Her voice was thin but laced with anger. Benteen had no doubt she would shoot if she felt threatened. The woman had the Winchester in her hands as they entered the camp. Benteen and Kendrick both kept their hands up.

'Like I said, we'll drop our guns, ma'am. We're just here to help. That man of yours looks to be in a bad way. We can help you get him to town.' Benteen kept his voice steady and his manner calm. The woman's expression was clear. She would fire in an instant.

'Won't do any good now,' the woman said. 'My brother here died during the night.'

Benteen glanced at the body. The man's face was turned into his blanket but the stillness told the tale. 'I'm mighty sorry, ma'am.'

The woman ignored him. 'Who do you ride for?'

'I don't ride for anyone, but Kendrick here works for Charles Nickles.'

At the mention of the name the woman swung the Winchester toward Kendrick, her eyes flashing with fury.

'He's not too fond of us homesteaders.'

'Take it easy, ma'am,' Kendrick said.

'You're one of the homesteaders?' Benteen asked, 'We thought they'd all been murdered.'

'Not hardly all. I'm Gloria Nash and this was my brother Lee. It was a Nickles rider that done this.' Her gaze never left Kendrick.

'Judas H. Priest!' Benteen was

stunned. 'Ma'am, we've got to get you to town. Nickles isn't behind this. It's a man named Walt Driggs, and maybe a few others. We're after Driggs. You won't be safe out here until we bring Driggs in.'

The woman returned her gaze to Benteen. 'I'm not going to town,' she said firmly.

'Ma'am, Walt Driggs is a dangerous man — '

'I'm a dangerous woman.'

With a start Benteen realized that the Winchester was now leveled at his chest. The woman appraised him, the fury still dancing in her eyes, but something else too. Her grief was etched plainly on her face, but he also recognized determination. This was quite a woman whom Benteen now faced. Benteen shrugged.

'Hell, I guess they make you womenfolk out here as tough as cowhide. Between you and Miss Deloney I'm lucky I haven't been shot yet.'

Gloria Nash raised an eyebrow.

'You've met Rebecca?'

'Took Dave Benson to her. He's mending under her care as we speak.'

'Dave Benson's alive? What about his wife and the girls?'

'Ma'am, we've got a lot to talk about.'

And in the next instant Gloria Nash stared hard into Hank Benteen's eyes and made up her mind. She lowered the Winchester. 'Put your hands down. I'll make some coffee.'

For the next hour they drank coffee and Benteen told Gloria Nash everything that occurred. Gloria Nash reciprocated by telling them of the attack that had eventually killed her brother. She had lost her husband to cholera three years earlier and had set out with her brother to start a new life west of the Mississippi. Nickles hadn't welcomed the homesteaders with open arms. But it was Walt Driggs and Mason Shrive who began harassing them.

'You can identify Shrive?' Benteen asked.

'I know him well enough. It was Driggs and Shrive.'

Benteen glanced at Kendrick. 'This will get them both hung.'

Kendrick nodded. Gloria Nash continued, 'They gave us an ultimatum. We refused, naturally. We'd been here two years already and none of us was about to leave.' She paused, her eyes misting. 'The day before we saw smoke in the direction of the Benson ranch. Lee armed himself. They came the next day. Lee was wounded but we'd prepared an escape route. They set fire to the cabin and we waited, choking on the smoke, but we managed to crawl into the creek that ran along the back. You know the rest.'

'You've been camped here since?' Kendrick asked.

'No, we've moved around. We were never certain whether they believed we perished in the fire. When they removed the burned timbers they should have realized there weren't any bones.'

'I don't think they know you

survived,' Benteen said. 'Do you know what happened to the Talbots?'

'They killed them all. They took their bodies to a gully about three miles from here. Lee and I heard the shooting and watched them bury the bodies. It was Shrive and Driggs.'

With Mason Shrive identified as an accomplice, Benteen wanted Gloria to return to Pitchstone with them. She refused. Gloria wanted to bury her brother on their property and rebuild the cabin. Benteen decided the wisest course of action was to appease her and help bury Lee Nash; in the meantime Kendrick would need to spread the word on Mason Shrive.

'Get word to Nickles,' Benteen said. 'And let Rebecca and Dave Benson know what has happened.'

'You can't just go out alone with a woman in this country,' Kendrick said, 'That's plain foolishness.'

'I'll handle it all right.' Benteen said.

Kendrick frowned but said no more. Before riding out Kendrick helped

Benteen wrap Lee's body in horse blankets and lash it to Gloria's horse. They tied her Winchester to the saddle with a leather cord lashed to the saddle ring. Then Kendrick tipped his hat to Gloria Nash and said to Benteen, 'See you later, gunslinger. Try and stay alive.'

They watched Kendrick ride away. Gloria was pensive as he rode off.

'That man is a killer,' she said at last.

'Yes, he is.'

'But you trust him?'

'I do. I knew him in Cheyenne. He won't break the law. He's honest but solid.'

'But he's still a killer.'

'He's killed when he's had to. I took him at his word. When I looked at him I figured him to be telling the truth. Yet a few days ago I half-expected him to ambush me. Sometimes the situation changes and we learn as we go along.'

An hour later Benteen and Gloria, riding on Benteen's horse, her arms about his waist, were making their way across the valley toward the barren land where Lee and Gloria had tried to start a new life. Gloria was stoic as they tied the horse carrying Lee's body to Benteen's mount. Benteen was alert and watching for any sign of Walt Driggs.

He enjoyed the way Gloria's arms gripped him around the waist and he cursed himself for having impure thoughts as they rode toward the site of her burned ranch. He held back some distance when the area came into view and he surveyed the landscape for signs of trouble. They dismounted and he decided to wait an hour before riding down to the site. They were on a tree-lined hill and the breeze was warm on their faces. Gloria's eyes shone brightly but Benteen admired the manner in which she held herself together. She had experienced an extraordinary amount of terror and anguish in a short time, just as the Bensons had and the Talbots, and now she had trusted her future to him. He wondered what that future would bring.

He felt he had to say something, find some way to help ease her suffering. When he turned to look at her she was already staring at him. He took in a breath.

'You picked a piece of heaven for your home,' he said. 'I don't think I've seen any finer country than this.'

It was all he could think of and he knew his words were inadequate, so he added: 'Ma'am, for whatever it's worth I'm sorry you had to go through these hard times.'

Her eyes were wet with tears and he turned away.

It was mid-afternoon when Benteen set to the grim task of digging another grave. When he was finished Gloria said a prayer over the mound and wept. Benteen politely walked away, allowing the woman a few moments alone with her grief. He wondered how in hell he'd become a gravedigger, but just as quickly brushed the thought aside. He was a Wind Rider, as the Sioux medicine man had told him. But then he recalled that the medicine man had also said his wanderings would cease once he found his shadow again.

He tried to recall the old man's exact words. 'Each man carries his shadow with him through life, and loses it only in death. When you accept that your shadow is linked to your boots the path will be easier to travel.'

Benteen knew there was more to the old man's words than Indian hokum put on for the white man's benefit, even if it did sound like words from one of Bill Cody's stage shows. He glanced over at Gloria and something stirred inside him. He wondered how old she was. Forty-five? Maybe a little older. No more than a few years younger than he. They weren't so old that they couldn't enjoy a few years together, make a go of the ranch.

So I've dug another grave, he thought, *and only the Talbots were wiped out. The other two families left survivors. I'll help them rebuild some-how.* He clenched his teeth, emotion boiling in his chest. Gloria came up to him and touched his elbow. He didn't want to look at her but she gently turned him around. Then her arms were around him and she held him briefly and wept some more. After a few seconds he nudged her aside.

He went to his saddle-bag and retrieved the biscuits Rebecca had given him. He wanted to think about something else, and food seemed like a good substitute. Gloria ate them gratefully, and then accepted water from Benteen's canteen.

'I never thought simple biscuits and water could taste so good,' she said.

'Can you show me where the Talbots are buried?' he asked.

'Yes. It's not far. Why is that important?'

'I need to know everything so Nickles can make his case. The tension in town is high. Nickles may not approve of you homesteaders, but he's no fool. These murders can turn the territory against him, especially now that we know two

124

of his men are behind it.'

They set out soon after and Gloria rode the horse that had carried her brother's body. Less than thirty minutes later she pointed to a small group of trees. Benteen was about to spur his horse for a closer look when something stopped him. It came to him on the breeze, a barely perceptible sound that only a man with his keen senses would pick up. The jangling of a spur, the rush of leather through an iron ring on a saddle, the clip-clop of an iron-shod hoof.

His gaze swept across the landscape. Dust behind them told of a rider following: that was the sound he'd heard. But there was something else. He squinted against the sun. Opposite their position a ridge of trees would make good cover for a man with a rifle. The instant he realized this the sun caught a barrel and revealed the shooter's position.

Wordlessly he reined his horse, and cantered into a cluster of pine. Gloria watched him without speaking. When they were safely behind the trees they dismounted.

'What is it?'

'A rider coming up fast behind us, and another man in the trees.'

Benteen's gun was already in his hand. He had palmed it before sliding from his saddle. Gloria untied her Winchester from its saddle ring. Benteen cast her an uncertain glance.

'I can shoot as well as any man,' she said in answer to his unspoken question.

Waiting was easy for Benteen, but he wondered how it was for the woman. There was no tension in him, only alertness. He slid his Colt back into his holster, his eyes taking in the landscape and his instinct evaluating everything that he saw, sensed, felt, heard or smelled. He was conscious of the dust kicked up by the approaching rider's horse, and even before the rider advanced he knew it was Jake Nickles. So keen were his senses that his eyes traced the outline of the horse and his mind evaluated the body structure. Something in that profile, still seen as a dark shape in the distance, convinced him of the rider's identity.

Then his mind turned to the man who he knew stood alone on that far ridge, obscured by pine tees, but watching and holding a rifle. Logic told him this was Walt Driggs. He hoped to confirm that hunch very soon.

How quickly events could change, he thought. A few days ago he was with Rebecca Deloney. Being in her proximity stirred old emotions. He missed his wife and he had come to somehow regret his life as a drifter. He was intent on seeing to it that Dave Benson and his girls were cared for, and now here he was tracking a killer in the mountains.

'Why did you holster your gun?'

Gloria's voice broke his reverie. She was beautiful and Benteen suddenly felt like a blushing schoolboy. He could only manage a quick glance at her before he had to look away.

'There's no immediate danger.'

'But you were ready for it, and you're still ready?'

'Yes.'

'What kind of man are you? A gunfighter?'

Benteen looked at her again. She was sincere, and perhaps a little concerned.

'I've been in gunfights, but I'm not a gunfighter.'

'What then? You don't have a stake in this. You can ride on and forget all this.'

Benteen felt her apprehension. She had suffered a great deal in a short time. He knew that sometimes grief and anxiety could tear a person apart.

'Ma'am, I'm not the enemy — '

'Call me Gloria.'

'All right, Gloria. It's like I told you earlier, I just rode into this valley. It wouldn't be very neighborly of me if I just rode on. A man helps when he can.'

'But you could have ridden on. It's not your fight.'

'Yes it is.'

Gloria was astounded. 'What do you mean? You don't owe any of us anything.'

Benteen thought hard on what to say next. She was persistent, and she wanted personal answers that he wasn't prepared to give. Still, she deserved an answer.

'It's like this, I reckon, I'm not a man that owns much. I've got a horse and a saddle, the clothes on my back, a rifle and this gun.' He tapped his holstered Colt. 'But what I own isn't all that I am. I have something else, like an idea inside, and I carry it with me. I mean that I should do right by others when I can. It's like my principle and I live by it.'

'You mean like a code of honor? I've read about such things. You're like one of those knights that served King Arthur in England.'

'I guess so, but it's not written down. It's just things that I know. This idea is like my code, as you call it, and that's who I am. As long as I have that idea

I'll do right by myself, and other folks, too.'

A softness came to her eyes and they misted a little. She gently placed her hand on his shoulder. 'I think I do understand now, and thank you.'

Benteen had to look away. The pain in her eyes, along with the gentleness and the compassion was almost too much for him to bear. After a moment he said, 'I reckon you can set down the rifle for a while. This rider has slowed down. It'll be a spell before he reaches us.'

They waited as the rider slowly approached, obviously scanning the trail for hoof marks. Fear has a scent of its own and Benteen smelled it now. It mingled on the wind with the scent of his horse, the pines, and the sagebrush. The boy — Jake Nickles, and Benteen could see him clearly now as he traversed an open stretch of ground — was frightened.

When he was 200 yards out Benteen said to Gloria, 'Stay here out of sight.

I'm going to try and save this kid's life.' With that Benteen stepped out from the security of the treeline and began walking toward Jake Nickles. When Jake saw him Benteen raised both hands. To his astonishment Jake reined his horse to a halt and raised his own hands. He began hollering at Benteen.

'For God's sake, don't shoot! Don't shoot! I don't mean you any harm! I just need to talk is all!'

Benteen approached the horse and grabbed the bridle. 'Easy, kid. I'm not going to shoot anyone. Can't you see my hands are in the air? What's this all about?'

The words rushed out, his eyes ablaze, spittle flicking from his lips. Benteen had never seen such a sight and he felt sorry for the kid as he unloaded his speech.

'Mr Benteen, I'm no gunfighter. It's just my father, goddamn it to hell, he's a hard man. Too hard. It's been difficult being his son and all, and I never much wanted to gun you anyway. I was just showing off for the boys. That and the whiskey, well . . . ' His voice trailed off as he watched Benteen and waited for a reaction. For his part, Benteen kept a stoic face. 'What I thought was, this thing about Walt Driggs, he pards with Mason Shrive, and I guess somehow those two are in cahoots. But I don't know why they did it.' Jake wiped his mouth with his sleeve. Talking so much made him nervous. Hell, Benteen's steely gaze made him nervous.

'Go on.' Benteen said. 'Say your piece. I don't have a quarrel with you and I reckon we can keep it that way.'

Jake let out a grateful sigh. 'What I'm trying to say is, Walt is a sick man. He's sick in the mind. But Mason is the one behind it all, although I can't prove it. But somehow Mason had a notion to get that land from those sodbusters.'

Benteen nodded. 'I figured as much.'

'And the thing is,' Jake continued, 'I have to help you stop them, and I have to help you prove it.'

'Does your father know you're here?'

'No sir.'

'Well, then Jake, if you get killed your father is bound to blame me and I don't need fifty of his riders out to gun me. You'll do as I say.'

'That's fair enough.' Jake was looking at Gloria. 'Who is she?' he asked.

'Miss Gloria Nash, meet Jake Nickles.'

'Nash? I thought you said they were all killed.'

'Thankfully I was wrong. She's taking me to the Talbot graves,' Benteen said, 'And you're coming with us.'

8

Benteen hadn't mentioned the rifleman who, he knew, was watching them. They skirted the valley and followed a trail through a stretch of small hills. Benteen knew he couldn't lose the rifleman but he took care to keep them from making an easy target. He had to keep Gloria and Jake alive. But an ambush was waiting for them, all the same, and he knew it.

They came to an area populated by tall evergreen and pines. The trees spread out over three hundred yards in the foothills. The treeline was broken on each side by some rocky hills, followed by yet another long stretch of forest.

'It's here,' Gloria said, gesturing toward a deer path. Benteen saw the wagon-wheel marks left in the dried mud.

They didn't go far. Fifty feet into the forest they found a Morgan wagon, still loaded with their cargo: the bloody tarpaulins that had carried the bodies.

'We watched them from those hills we passed,' Gloria said. 'Mason Shrive watched as Driggs did most of the work.'

Benteen dismounted, reins in hand, and examined the wagons. They'd made a cursory effort to cover the wagon with deadfall and leaves. Leaving the wagon but taking the horses when they left meant they'd intended to return. It was a mad scheme, and the more he thought about it the more perplexed he became. His horse resisted, stomped a hoof. 'Easy now. I'm pondering things. Let me have at it.' Benteen said.

'Who are you talking to?'

Gloria was watching him with a quizzical expression.

Benteen blushed and turned his face away. 'I was talking to my horse. I guess it's a bad habit I picked up along the trail.'

Gloria giggled: a light musical laugh. 'My pa did that with his plow horses. He talked with his horses all day when he was plowing the fields. He said a man that talks to horses is either wise or foolish, depending on your point of view.'

Benteen looked back at Gloria. There was no malice in her features, no concern that he was a loony sun-baked trail rider. She was serious.

'Is that so?' Benteen said. 'Well, I reckon your father was a wise man.'

'Yes he was,' Gloria said and smiled. 'And I've always trusted a man who knows how to handle horses.'

Benteen was about to answer when the first shot clipped the bark off a tree. A second later they heard the rifle's crack and Benteen yelled, 'Get off your horses!' Gloria and Jake dismounted.

'Grab the reins and follow me! Quick!' Benteen led them along a deer path that cut into the pine forest. The trees would block the gunman's view.

'It's gotta be Driggs!' Jake said. The

kid was anxious, his eyes darting back and forth.

'Hold up a minute,' Benteen said. He knew he had to keep them calm. 'That's only one rifleman out there. I'd figured he was watching us. He made a mistake and fired too soon. He must be nervous as hell. You two hunker down here. Keep the horses calm.' He looked at Gloria. 'Talk to the horses if you have to, especially if shooting starts.' He smiled and Gloria appeared to be reassured.

'You gonna leave us here!?' Jake blurted.

'Only until I look around. I'll be up by the treeline, but on the ground. Just stay here. I'll be right back.'

He moved into the underbrush and remembered a day like this, years past, outside Gettysburg. He had that same expectant feeling knowing that those Southern rebels would try to cut him down with their rifles. His pulse was thrumming and his mouth was dry. He inched forward and peered through the thickets.

The rifleman had to be on the right. A scattering of trees offered him cover and the incline gave him the advantage of being on high ground. Benteen surveyed the valley another moment and made his decision.

He backed off and returned to the clearing. 'We're going around,' he announced flatly. 'I want to circle the valley and get on higher ground. That'll take us across the valley and closer to Pitchstone.'

'Yes, that might take a full day.' Jake said glumly. 'What if he follows us?'

'It will take a full day, but we have grub. And he will follow us but not right away. When the shooting starts we'll be better off up on those switchbacks.'

They set out through the trees, walking their horses. An hour later, when the trail cleared, they mounted their horses and began the ascent into the foothills circling the valley. In the late afternoon the sky turned black and Benteen watched the storm clouds churning over the western ridge of mountains. The wind brought him the smell of rain as lightning began to snap along the horizon.

They followed an arroyo until they found a place where the rocks and small trees made a canopy against the rain. They made camp. Benteen and Jake went to work making a lean-to from evergreen branches. They hunkered down in a depression of rocks, the evergreen branches partly covering them. Gloria was exhausted and immediately fell asleep.

Benteen busied himself cleaning his Winchester. It was a nervous habit but he accomplished it without appearing nervous. Jake eyed him glumly.

'You think we'll make it?' he asked.

'We'll make it all right. I'll take the first watch. You might want to get some shut-eye.'

'Yeah.' Jake crossed his arms and settled down. After a few minutes he said, 'It was the whiskey talking that night I pulled my gun on you.'

'I know that. You don't have to worry about it.'

'The thing is, I came out here to help make it right, but now it seems to be worse.'

'The difference is this time you made the right decision,' Benteen said. 'All a man has sometimes is his word. If you're good for that then you've got a lot.'

Jake looked at Benteen. Then, exhausted, he stared off into the distance. Benteen let him be. The kid was trying to do the right thing but getting back to Pitchstone might be a chore. They both knew it without saying it.

Benteen wanted to get the guns cleaned before they made their way back to Pitchstone. He cleaned the Winchester first because it was the easiest; then he used his bandanna to wipe the cartridges clean. He jacked the lever several times, confident it was clear and wouldn't jam.

He looked at Gloria. Her eyelids were fluttering and in another moment she would be awake. In the late-afternoon light, even with the sky shadowed by an approaching storm, her skin had a glow to it. Her face was a pale pink which seemed all the more lovely because of the red tint in her hair. Looking at her reminded him somehow of a garden of pale roses.

She opened her eyes and looked at him and her eyes were soft and blue. In that moment he wanted to touch her face, to trace his fingers along her mouth and gently brush the leaves from her hair. Something soft broke open inside him. She saw it in his eyes but she didn't move. They watched each other for another moment, until Benteen said, 'You have a leaf in your hair.'

'Oh.' Her hand reached up and pulled the leaf from a tangle of hair. She studied it a moment as if memorizing its every contour. She stretched and got up, averting her eyes from his.

'How long did I sleep?'

'Not long. I cleaned the guns.'

She looked at the sky. 'This isn't good.'

He followed her gaze to the north-west. The horizon was thick with mist and a boiling mass of purple clouds where lightning spit at the earth like the exploring tongues of serpents.

'That storm could delay us longer than you thought,' she said.

'Let's hope it slows Driggs down, too,' Benteen said. 'The best we can do is go as far as we can, try and get close to Pitchstone. When we work our way south around these switchbacks there's more trees, and a lake.'

It began to rain. At first the rain was soft, caressing them, and it felt good to let the wetness wash away the grime that clung to them after their long ride. But in a little while the rain turned cold and the muffled sound of thunder beyond the distant peaks warned them that the storm was raging closer.

Benteen remembered a day, when he was a boy, the kids were making their way home from school and an unex-pected storm caught them by surprise.

They ran for shelter in a nearby barn, but one boy stayed out in the rain. When the rain was too fierce he took shelter under an old giant oak. The sky was like a solid gray wall and the rain was coming down so hard it stung like a bee. He watched with the other children as the lightning split open the gray wall of sky, sent a tendril of blazing light at the tree, and when they blinked the boy was on the ground, dead, smoke curling up from his ruffled hair.

The lean-to was sufficient for Benteen's purpose. They were relatively safe while they were pressed against the hillside, but the evergreen branches did little to protect them. They were soaked in minutes.

'What good are these damn branches?' Jake said irritably.

'They keep us covered from prying eyes,' Benteen answered.

Jake settled back again, pulling his hat over his face.

For a while there was nothing but the sound of the rain and wind. Gloria had picked up the Winchester and was holding it across her chest like a staff. She didn't say anything, the two of them just looked at each other in the rain. The rain matted her hair to her head and little beads of water formed in her hair like small jewels. Without thinking he brushed the water from her brow and that was when she kissed him. Then she dropped her head on to his chest and held him and they didn't say anything for a long time. That was nice, to be kissed, he thought, a nice thing to happen after coming so close to death. He wanted to kiss her again. Benteen was trembling slightly from the cold and it wasn't easy to convince himself that he had a future. Not with the cold rain pouring down and Walt Driggs roaming the countryside.

The afternoon passed slowly. She slept for a while in his arms. She was hungry but never complained. He liked that. Complaining only made the hunger worse. If he thought about the time it made the minutes drag by slowly. Don't think about anything, he told himself. He had done this before and with practice had acquired the skill. But at those times when he had to survive in the wilderness he hadn't had a pretty woman in his arms, and now all he could think about was her softness.

An image of Rebecca Deloney flashed through his mind. He was quite taken with her. Then he recalled the words of the Sioux medicine man, telling him that one day the wind would push him into the path of a *wicin*, a girl, and the path of the *sungmanitu tanka*, the wolf who followed the wind, would blend into the shadows.

What the hell had that meant? That he would settle down again? It seemed impossible to him, and the long years had been difficult. Still, the Sioux had been right. The wind had pushed him gently into this valley and into the paths of two women. Emotion blazed in his chest and he felt that he might be on the verge of something new and exciting. But he also had to think about

Walt Driggs and Mason Shrive. Driggs would be following their trail once he realized they'd gone into the hills. He couldn't afford to let them reach Pitchstone. It would be a race now that the storm had slowed them down. The night passed slowly. While Gloria and Jake slept Benteen thought through all that had occurred and resolved to finish it without harm to Gloria and Jake. They were the key now.

They were awake before sunrise and the rain had diminished to a light drizzle. The mountains during a thunderstorm are like another world. Few have the skills and willpower needed to survive the brutal forces of nature that constantly lashed at them. But Benteen had survived in mountains before and he reveled in the majestic powers of nature. The land was uncaring but offered its beauty as reward for those strong enough to live through a storm.

The mountain peaks had disappeared into a gray fog. Sometimes the mountains would disappear altogether, only to reappear days later. To the Sioux they were gods awakening to a new day. The tall trees towered like sentinels in the mist. Occasionally the dark shape of a hawk or an eagle would flap from the trees and circle on the wind before vanishing into the netherworld of fog and mist that hung like a thin curtain in every direction.

So they proceeded to ride; their horses clopped obediently forward and the riders progressed, wary of danger but optimistic with Hank Benteen leading them to safety. They were higher on the switchbacks when Benteen looked behind them and saw two riders, about a hundred yards apart. He hadn't expected two riders, and they didn't appear to be together. The further rider was traveling slowly. Benteen only had the one glimpse, but it was enough.

Jake sensed the tension in him and followed his eyes.

'What is it?'

'Riders behind us.'

'Riders? More than one?'

'Get movin'.'

They moved silently and quickly. Benteen wanted to get to higher ground but once they moved past the scrub there was little cover. He wanted to move higher but away from the riders. They still had time because he didn't think they'd been seen. They went over a rocky plateau, keeping low, and moving quickly to avoid being spotted. Then they rode down a gully where a steady stream of water rushed along with them, sloshing up on to their legs. Up again on to the rocks, Benteen's hand dropping to his holstered Colt as instinct took over and sent a warning through him. He saw them thirty yards away on a switchback just as the closest rider saw them.

Now we'll see what I can do against two men, Benteen thought grimly. There was no place they could go to hide. Driggs must have traveled through the dark on a hunch he could catch up with them. It was a dangerous and foolish move, but it had worked. Now it was a matter of finding the right position.

'What do we do?' Jake asked.

'We have to fight now. There's no sense in running and this place is as good as any.'

The two riders split off, one to the right and one to the left. The closer rider held position thirty yards in front of them, watching intently. Benteen knew it was Driggs. They dismounted and Benteen pulled the Winchester from his saddle boot.

They watched in amazement as the further rider spurred his horse and closed in on the other man. They saw the man point his Colt and Benteen saw the muzzle flash a split second before the sound reached his ears. The gunshot echoed dully off the rocks. The shot missed and the other man turned and scrambled for cover. Both men fired furiously at each other, the flurry of gunshots popping like firecrackers, and the man on horseback fell, his Colt falling uselessly from his hand.

In that instant Benteen realized that John Kendrick hadn't gone back to town. He notched the Winchester in his shoulder and sighted on Driggs. His finger curled on the trigger and he felt the cold metal on his skin. He prayed he didn't slip on the wet rocks when he fired. Driggs was about to spur his horse when he fired. The Winchester barked and Driggs fell from his saddle as his horse whinnied and snorted in fear, rearing on its hindlegs as the man thumped on to the rocks like a sack of grain.

Then Benteen was running with the rifle snap still echoing off the canyon walls. Driggs was on his feet. Benteen saw a splash of red on his arm. He fired again, missed, but by now Driggs had pulled himself back on to his horse. With a mad scream Driggs spurred his horse and galloped down the trail.

'Damn!' Benteen grunted. Driggs was out of sight. Jake and Gloria came up beside him, the fear showing plainly on their faces.

'That's Kendrick,' Benteen announced. 'Let's go see if he's still alive.'

Kendrick was on his back and still breathing. His eyes fluttered opened when Benteen leaned over him. There were two bullet wounds in his chest. He coughed blood.

'Almost . . . ' Kendrick gasped and coughed again. 'Almost . . . had . . . him . . . ' His voice trailed off.

'You did right.' Benteen said, 'Wish I'd known you were riding our back-trail.'

'No time . . . saw Driggs . . . on . . . the . . . way . . . back . . . '

He coughed again, blood dribbling from his mouth.

'Careful . . . ' Kendrick whispered, 'He's . . . as . . . loco . . . as . . . they . . . come . . . '

His eyes rolled back and his body shivered once as he died.

Benteen had Jake stand guard with the Winchester while he covered Kendrick's body with rocks. It took the better part of two hours to cover the body. Gloria helped as much as possible, which impressed Benteen. She scrounged for rocks and small boulders and hauled them to the body along with Benteen. When Jake protested Benteen growled at him to watch and listen. When they finished Benteen removed his hat and said over the grave, 'Ride to a better place, pard.' Then he put his hat on and mounted his horse.

Jake said, 'You're not much for sentiment, are you?'

Benteen's steely eyes squinted at the kid. 'I'll be sentimental as hell when I'm dead.'

Gloria frowned but said nothing.

They rode a few miles, all the while Benteen wondering where Driggs had gone. He didn't think that the bullet wound on his arm would stop him. Kendrick's dying warning was very much on his mind. The last thing a man should do is corner a wounded animal.

They rose higher into the hills following a faint trail only deer might follow. By now they had circled half the valley, but the last half would be just as dangerous. And then they had to descend and cross the northern section of the valley's floor.

Suddenly Benteen heard the clopping of hoofs on rock and Walt Driggs came up on the right, his arm swinging a rifle to aim. Benteen pulled his Colt and fired knowing he would miss, but it frightened Driggs and gave him time to rein to the side.

The gunshot spooked Gloria's horse and it bolted into the trees.

'After her!' he shouted at Jake. The kid slammed his spurs into his horse's flanks as Benteen fired again, swinging around quickly and aiming for Driggs.

Driggs was laughing, already having raced out of view. But Benteen could hear him chucking like a maniac. A chill ran down his spine. He reined his horse and set out after Gloria.

Jake had Gloria's horse by the reins and they were waiting quietly in a small grove of saplings. Jake's face shone with perspiration, the nervousness shining in his eyes. Gloria was pale, but otherwise stoic.

'We need to kill him!' Jake said, licking his lips. 'Or he's gonna hound us into our graves. That man is insane.'

Jake was right. Driggs was out of control, wounded and panicking. He could stand and fight but one or more of them would surely die.

'Take it easy and follow me,' Benteen said hoarsely.

They cut up a shelf of rock and emerged on a plateau overlooking the lake. He could see the place far below where they had spent the night. Rain made circles on the water as a cold wind came up with the scent of more rain.

Driggs was coming. Benteen could feel it. More appropriately, the wind carried the whisper of sound — leather creaking, an iron-shod hoof striking the muddy trail.

He held the horse steady, skirting the ledge, looking for a way down. It was plain to him they had to jump but he feared the horse might hesitate. He brought the horse up to the ledge twice to give him the idea. Another moment and Driggs would ride out of the forest, so it had to be now.

Benteen turned his head to Gloria and Jake and said 'We're going over. Hang on tight and when we hit the water swim back toward this cliff.'

'You're crazy!' Jake nearly screamed. 'We can't jump our horses off a cliff!'

'Trust me, kid. These horses can swim better than I can.'

Before Jake could protest he cantered around and slapped Jake's horse on the rump. Benteen blocked the horse with his own mount and then he pulled his Colt and fired a shot at its feet. The horse reared and jumped. Jake screamed as they went over.

Gloria was already preparing herself. She trotted her mount back, then set herself to gallop forward as they heard the splash as Jake and his horse hit the water.

Gloria paused and looked at Benteen. 'I needed a bath anyway,' she said and smiled. Benteen was so surprised he didn't have time to respond as Gloria spurred her horse and leaped from the cliff.

He was beginning to spur the horse when he heard a whinny and the sharp clop of a hoof on stone. He turned and saw Driggs coming up the trail. He felt a small satisfaction at having eluded him again, and by the time he thought this Gloria and her horse were splashing into the lake. Benteen dug his spurs into his horse. The horse whinnied loudly and jumped; they galloped in the air before they slammed into the lake. Benteen felt his breath forced from his lungs. He thought he heard a gunshot as he fell. Then the water was filling his lungs and he was drowning. He flailed his arms to slow his momentum but something was pulling him down. Panic seized him as he realized his boot was caught in a stirrup. He had fallen from his horse and was thrashing upside down in the water.

His fingers were numb from the cold

water and the shock of the fall had taken much of his energy. He fumbled with the stirrup, bending over to pry at his boot. He realized they were still spinning slightly, dropping deeper into the lake. That wasn't right. His horse should have broken the surface quickly and gone instinctively to the shore. Then he saw the silhouette of the horse's head, the mane fanned like an old woman's hair, a stream of blood bubbling from a gaping hole on the neck. The bullet meant for him had taken his horse's life.

He twisted his leg free and extended his arms, clawing at the surface. His lungs were burning. He scratched his way upward, peering through the murky depths. He couldn't judge how far he'd sunk but he thought the surface had to be near.

He broke the surface gasping. A moment passed before he could get his bearings. The water was choppy from the breeze and he settled himself into a routine of cupping water with his palms and kicking his legs to stay afloat. He was relieved to see Gloria and Jake already on the shore. He treaded water, rocking in the gentle swells, his eyes scanning the rim for any sign of Driggs. He swam toward shore, pulled himself on to the ground and lay there breathing heavily.

'Made it again.' he said, forcing a smile as Gloria rushed to his side.

'We can't stay here,' Jake said. 'Driggs is up on those rocks. Without Benteen's horse one of us will have to walk. We can switch off every hour. You two can ride double to start.' Benteen was surprised when Jake grabbed his arm and pulled him to his feet. The kid had some brass and was learning quick enough. Gloria was shivering but her eyes showed concern for Benteen, not herself.

'I thought for a moment . . . ' she began.

Benteen shrugged. 'My horse took the bullet. Jake is right, we can't stay here.'

Once more they moved into the trees. Benteen looked back once at the cliff above the lake where a solitary dark figure stood like a sentry on the precipice. And the wind carried a sound like a screeching banshee as the shivering and exhausted trio disappeared into the forest.

9

For the second time Benteen rode into Pitchstone under the scrutiny of the townspeople. They filled the boardwalk on both sides of the street, a murmur running through the crowd. Hank Benteen rode with Gloria Nash holding her arms around his waist and Jake Nickles following.

Rebecca and Dave Benson came out of the restaurant to watch. Benson still looked pale but the fact that he was up and walking was heartening. Charles Nickles came out of the hotel as they dismounted at the hitching post. Rebecca crossed the street, gushing over Gloria.

'Miss Nash! I guess this is a miracle . . . You must be hungry . . . ' she hesitated, glancing at Benteen. 'We'll get you a nice bath and some food.' She turned to Benteen and Jake. 'And come over to eat when things settle down,' she said. 'And then you can tell us all about it.'

Tears came to Gloria's eyes and the two women hugged. Benteen felt something warm come alive inside his chest and he had to hold his emotions in check. He held himself rigid, an impassive figure as the women walked away. Jake stood next to him, visibly nervous. And no wonder, Benteen thought, because Charles Nickles had set his cold, hazel eyes on them, his presence emitting an air of expectancy and authority.

Nickles pulled a gold watch from his pocket and snapped it open, glanced at it, and returned it to its pocket.

'It's one o'clock,' Nickles said matter-of-factly. 'Let's have a drink before you clean up.' He strode purposefully to the saloon and they followed him. This time Nickles was content to allow people to remain within earshot, although Benteen noticed the crowd gave him a wide berth. Benteen was acutely aware that Mason Shrive was nowhere to be seen.

Exhausted, they sat at a table and immediately the barman set a glass of beer and a tumbler of whiskey before each of them. Benteen drank the whiskey, savoring the warmth as it spread through his belly. He drank half his beer in one gulp and Jake did the same. The elder Nickles watched patiently, sipping his own whiskey. After some minutes Benteen told him what had happened, taking his time as he told it and leaving nothing out. When he was finished Benteen said, 'Jake here did all right. Hauled me to my feet after I drank half that lake.'

Nickles looked at his son, the pride visible on his face, but instead of complimenting the youngster he said: 'Kendrick was a good man. I'm sorry he didn't make it. I'll make inquiries as to his family.' Then he set his whiskey down and added, 'While you were gone I spoke with Dave Benson.'

Benteen was surprised.

'I offered to rebuild his ranch, and I'll do the same for the Nash woman,' Nickles continued. 'I'm not going to allow this problem to turn into a war. Maybe that'll happen in other parts of the state, but it won't happen here.'

'That's a generous offer,' Benteen said. 'I expect that news was well received by Benson?'

'It was. I've drawn up a contract and I'll pay him in cattle when my herds graze on his land. A family's hunger can be easily satisfied by a few herd now and again. The Talbot parcel can be divided between the two. I'll not have my reputation sullied by people who can't agree. I've spent forty-five years building my business and by God almighty I'll not see this territory turned into a haven for lawless owlhoots!' Nickles finished his whiskey and gestured to Joe Driscoll who was leaning against the bar. 'Joe, put out word I'm offering a two-thousand dollar reward for Shrive and Driggs, dead or alive, and I'll pay in gold coin.'

163

Driscoll went from the saloon, a murmur rippling through the crowd that pressed in around them. All ears were keen to hear everything being said, and both Nickles and Benteen were aware that territorial history was being made by their actions. They finished their drinks and the barman silently brought a fresh round. Jake looked as if the drinks were taking effect as he appeared more relaxed. Still, Benteen noticed that the elder Nickles had not spoken directly to his son since their return.

The tall rancher sipped his whiskey, his face glowing with purpose. 'It was a mad scheme,' he said. 'And I want it made clear that I don't condone the actions of outlaws. Any man who works for me knows I have my own code, as all good men must, and I don't settle my differences with gunplay unless it's a last resort. Shrive and Driggs will be hunted to the ends of the earth if necessary. There's not a corner they can hide in. You all listening had best mark my words.'

And indeed they did. All present knew of the man's ferocity and none doubted that Shrive or Driggs would be brought to justice. The only question was how long would they elude their fate? Suddenly Benteen was tired, as tired as he had been in years. It was the beer and whiskey, of course, combined with his exertions. Damn it all! He was getting long in the tooth. Then he thought about Gloria kissing him, and he thought about the sleek, pretty form of Rebecca Deloney and he cursed himself silently for drinking too quickly. A man's mind could easily get rattled by women and booze.

'You have a job with me any time you wish,' Nickles was saying. 'I'll pay you the best wage you've ever earned as a cowpuncher.'

'I appreciate that,' Benteen said. 'But I reckon I haven't thought much about where I'll go next.'

'At least allow me to buy you a new horse. And your Winchester was in the saddle boot when your horse went down, isn't that right?'

'I reckon so . . . ' Benteen began.

'Then it's settled. I'll replace the Winchester and I'll buy you a new set of clothes and all the cartridges you want, too. By God, man, don't turn me down. I'd be insulted.'

'Well, Mr Nickles, that says it plainly enough. I won't turn you down. And I'm especially grateful for a horse.' Benteen took a long swallow of his beer. He ran his hand through his long hair. 'And I guess I lost my hat in that lake as well. I'm obliged to you.'

'It's settled, by God. Within the hour you'll have an account over at the dry-goods store and I'll have a horse waiting for you tomorrow at the stables, fully equipped with a new saddle. But in the meantime get yourself some new clothes.'

Benteen rose and shook Nickles's hand. 'Fine, now I need to clean up before I check in with those gals at the restaurant. Good day, Mr Nickles.'

Benteen had taken a few steps when

something crossed his mind. He turned back to Nickles and said, 'And like I said, Jake here did fine. I'm obliged to him as well. I couldn't ask for a better saddle pal.'

Nickles nodded but still remained silent. He was a hard man, after all, Benteen thought as he strode from the saloon.

★   ★   ★

Benteen checked into the hotel. Rebecca wouldn't need him bunking at the restaurant now that she'd taken Gloria under her wing. He ordered a bath be drawn up; when it was ready he sat in the cast-iron tub in the hotel's bathroom and smoked while he pondered the turn of events. He was thinking again how circumstances had altered his life and how quickly he had developed a sense of responsibility to the people he'd met since riding into this valley. Not many days ago he had been a drifter, just another cowboy on his way to find more work.

Later he picked out some new clothes at the store. He hadn't bought new clothes in over eighteen months and he reckoned he was overdue. His shirt had become threadbare. He found a cream-colored Stetson that fit as well as his old one, some checkered shirts and some dungarees. The clerk, a pleasant man named Newman, asked him if he might need a belt or boots as well. Benteen realized his bill was being paid by Nickles and the clerk wanted him to purchase as much as he could carry. But Benteen wouldn't take more than he needed. His boots had held up. They had been made in Texas from the finest leather and there wasn't any reason to buy new ones. He did choose a belt, which pleased Newman.

He took the clothes back to the hotel and tried them on. It felt good to be wearing clean clothes but when he looked at himself in the mirror above the bureau he was shocked. He hadn't shaved in a week and his long hair hung over his eyes. He looked like a tired old mountain man. When he thought about Gloria he rubbed his bristled jaw self-consciously. He thought about facing Gloria and Rebecca down at the restaurant and he decided he'd better shave. But when he strapped on his gunbelt he felt soiled.

He stood looking at himself in the mirror without moving. A shave and a haircut would do it, he thought, but the familiar weight on his right hip was out of place. The old leather holster and scarred Colt didn't feel right any longer, but leaving the gun behind was out of the question. Shrive and Driggs would always be a threat. Only death would stop them now, and their fate would be decided soon enough. Nickles would have his men scouring the country for them. Still, Benteen's experience had taught him to expect the unexpected.

He decided to clean the gun. He sat on the bed and removed the base pin and cylinder. He cleaned them with an oily cloth he'd kept in his saddle-bag. He wiped off the cartridges that had been resting in the cylinder, then cleaned the muzzle and ejection spring. He used a small tin of oil and lubricated the blue metal. The gun was in good shape considering what it had been through. There wasn't any rust visible, which had been his chief concern. The rain and swim in the lake might have a detrimental effect on the metal later, but he was satisfied that the gun wasn't compromised yet. It felt good in his hand. He reloaded, easing the hammer down on an empty cylinder. But again, when he strapped the gun-belt around his waist he felt unclean.

Benteen knew what the problem was then, although he couldn't yet quite put it into words. He went down to visit the barber. Sam O'Brien greeted him cheerily which reminded Benteen of the day he rode into Pitchstone, when he had been greeted by a very different reception. On that day he had been viewed with suspicion if not scorn by all those who lined up along the boardwalk to watch him. O'Brien cut his hair and chattered about cattle prices. When he was finished Benteen paid him and O'Brien said, 'You have a nice afternoon, Mr Benteen.' It was as if they were friends although they'd only just met. The friendly tone and the small talk was all in stark contrast to a life on the trail where your destination was determined by the wind.

He returned to his room and again examined himself in the mirror. He didn't recognize himself. He wondered if he was handsome. Then he wondered why it mattered. He sat wearily on the bed, his hand dropping to his Colt. He unbuckled his gunbelt and looked at it. He knew what the problem was. He wanted to be done with this tool. He wanted something else. The Colt had saved his life countless times, just as it had taken the lives of many bad men, but now he wanted to set it aside. He'd relied on his expertise with a gun too many times.

Fatigue settled on him and his shoulders slumped. That had been one hell of a ride with Gloria and Jake. He was hungry but he knew he needed some sleep. He would let it happen while he pondered things. His mind was awash with images and ideas and he needed some quiet time to sort things out.

He settled back against the headboard, his hand automatically sliding the Colt from the holster, the gunbelt tumbling to the floor. How many times had he slept like this, with a gun in his hand? He turned his head and looked at the window. The thin, blue-lace curtains ruffled briefly from a breeze. Through the thin fabric the sky was still bright although the shadows were beginning to lengthen. He could sleep for an hour or more and then go have dinner. He wanted to see Gloria and Rebecca and Dave Benson and his children.

He closed his eyes momentarily, adrift between sleeping and dreaming, and just before he was pulled under the image of Gloria kissing him flashed through his mind. Then he slept heavily before following the dream trail the Sioux claimed was as real as this earth. It was a strange dream. He was on horseback down in the valley where the homesteaders had tried to build new lives. It was nearing sunset and the sky's fire blazed like a gold coin against a sky awash in turquoise and orange. The wind had picked up and a thousand leaves whispered with movement, their branches beckoning to him from every direction. He sat astride his horse but was uncertain which direction he should follow. The soft afternoon light saturated the land and for the first time in years he felt no sense of urgency to keep riding. The mountains towered majestically along the horizon, the peaks and valleys offering bountiful game. Their beauty alone held him steadfast in wonderment.

The scent of sagebrush and wildflowers drifted along the breeze. His horse nickered and nibbled at the meadow grass. He dismounted and swept his gaze along the ridges and jagged treeline. When the sun touched the mountains the shadows began to lengthen, but so too did the colors deepen. It was as if this was the moment of creation and he alone stood amidst the blessing of a life rich with color and sound. He marveled at the small, yellow flowers that dotted the meadow, the birdsong that drifted from the pine and oak trees.

How sacred was this land and this country to him then. He was no longer forlorn and angry, but a sense of peace filled his very soul. A painter could set up his easel on this very spot and spend a lifetime painting the landscape because it changed so dramatically every few moments. As the light changed by the sun's position the mountains changed, too, and the amber palette glowed with violet one moment, or rich brown, green and yellow the next. And the breeze carried the scent of pine and musty earth and the clear, fresh scent of mountain water trickling from the rocks and into the springs and rivers.

The sun melted behind the peaks, one last ray of light splitting the air like a glimmering sword, and twilight presumed to take its place among the mountains, hills and valleys. He stood transfixed as the world was transformed before him, then he saw the riders in the distance. They were tall, dark figures on horseback, black cloaks flapping like wings behind them, their steeds black as coal and breathing flame. As the riders drew near he saw their faces were those of grinning skulls, eyes ablaze with an unholy light.

He awoke with a start. The room was dark. He lay absolutely still listening for sounds in the darkness. He felt his heart beating loudly. As his eyes adjusted to the dark he could discern light outside the curtained window, a reflection of the light filtering up from the shops along the boardwalk. Instinctively his thumb pressed against the hammer, his finger curling about the trigger. The gun was cold and heavy in his hand.

From downstairs he could hear a muffled voice followed by what he deemed was a woman's laughter. Had he locked the door? He couldn't remember, but he was satisfied that he was alone in the room. Still, the dream had been haunting. He sat up and swung his legs off the bed. He allowed himself another ten minutes just listening. The Sioux had told him long ago that dreams held portents of things to come; they were messages from the great Spirits that a man should heed. At that moment Benteen didn't find anything fanciful about the Sioux beliefs. Most men dismissed such talk as flights of fancy but not Benteen. Death was coming. He had beaten death before and if he was to survive one last battle he had to face it with a clear mind.

When he was ready he stood up. He flicked a wooden match to flame and lit the oil lamp on the bureau. The wick sputtered to life bathing the room in a warm glow. He twisted the metal pin until the wick was set midway. He wanted the wick to burn down until the light was but a faint glow when he returned. He holstered his gun, the feeling of unseemliness now vanished.

William Fleming, the hotel owner, was on duty at the desk. Benteen nodded to him as the man said, 'Good evening, sir.' Hell, I'm getting to know a corral full of people, Benteen thought. The store clerk, the barber, the hotel proprietor — he knew them all by name now.

He stopped on the boardwalk outside the hotel and then moved into the shadows away from the backlit doorway. He paused and observed the dark street. A dozen places could hide a gunman. He peered into the darkness and shadows moved among shadows. It could be anything, he thought. He stepped out into the diffused light that pooled on the street, his ears straining to hear the *click* of a hammer being pulled back. Nothing. He moved on with a shrug. If not tonight then the next one, or the one after.

When he entered the restaurant Rebecca looked up and smiled. She came to him hurriedly. 'Why, Hank, I was wondering when you'd come.'

'I fell asleep. I guess I'm a little old to be riding about the mountains.'

'You're not old at all,' she said enthusiastically. 'And I know a woman who's been waiting on you.' Rebecca offered another sweet smile. 'Gloria hasn't taken her dinner yet. She was hoping to sit down with you.'

She studied his face for a reaction and he felt the weight of her scrutiny.

Hank thought, why not? He allowed himself to smile and reveal his feelings.

'That's real fine,' he said amiably. 'I was hoping for the same. She's quite a lady.'

He sat down while Rebecca bustled away. In a moment Gloria came out of the kitchen. She took the chair opposite him as he stood up and went to remove his hat.

'Keep your hat on, please,' Gloria said. 'We don't have to be so formal after all we've been through.'

Hank sat down but removed his hat all the same and let it dangle on the post of an empty chair.

'I have to say the haircut and shave are an improvement,' Gloria said. 'Why, you look downright dapper!'

Benteen wondered if he was blushing. Suddenly he felt warm around the collar. Gloria's eyes shone with merriment and warmth. She wore a blue cotton dress. He thought blue suited her perfectly. Gloria was also conscious of Benteen's gaze and her hand instinctively brushed a strand of hair from her forehead.

'I was grateful for a hot bath, too,' she said. 'Rebecca has been so helpful. She bought me this dress.'

'It's a nice dress,' Benteen said. Her hair had been combed out and in the soft glow of the oil lamp it sparkled with color. Her skin had a warm sheen that again reminded him of pale roses.

Rebecca came back into the room with their food. There were steak and potatoes and carrots and coffee. Benteen cut into his steak greedily. They ate without speaking, each of them intent on satiating their hunger. The restaurant was nearly full and Elma and Rebecca were busy taking care of their customers. The room was filled with the murmur of conversation, the clatter of forks and knives against the plates. Benteen relaxed a little, but he never let his eyes drift far from the door. He was aware of all who came and went. When they were finished Elma took away the dishes and Rebecca brought them each a slice of apple pie.

'This looks delicious.' Benteen said.

'Of course it is,' Gloria said. 'Rebecca's the best cook in Wyoming.'

'I'd have to agree with that.'

'Now you two just enjoy it,' Rebecca said happily. 'Come about August I'll make my apple pie with fresh fruit instead of these canned apples.' Then Rebecca looked at Benteen and asked, 'Do you mind if Dave Benson and his girls join you?'

'Not at all. I was hoping to see them.'

A few moments later Dave and the two girls were sharing apple pie with Benteen and Gloria, and Benteen experienced a rare feeling of camaraderie. He was enjoying himself. The two little girls were beautiful, smiling and apparently happy. Rebecca kept an eye on their table while Elma handled the late patrons coming in for dinner. Dave Benson was still thin, but he was moving about easily. Benteen knew it wouldn't be long now and the gauntness would vanish thanks to Rebecca's cooking. The man was lucky to be alive.

'Mr Nickles has offered to rebuild the ranches,' Benson said. 'Do you think I can trust the man?'

The question surprised Benteen, but then after a moment's reflection he realized he'd be asking the same thing should he have experienced Benson's tragedy.

'I expect so,' Benteen said. 'He doesn't want his name dragged into the mud. I expect he'll do right by you. Half of Wyoming has heard about all of this and he won't go back on his word.'

Benteen repeated his account of the last few days, knowing that Gloria and others had already spoken with him, but Benson would want to hear it all directly from him. When he was finished Benson frowned.

'I expect Shrive and Driggs are in the Dakotas by now, or well across Utah or Colorado, depending on their direction.'

'I doubt it,' Benteen said.

The table fell silent. Rebecca set down a handful of dishes and pulled up a chair next to Benson. The murmur of conversation in the restaurant diminished as everyone waited for Benteen's next words. He glanced around the room. There was no hostility here, only curiosity, and perhaps a trace of worry.

'They won't let this go,' he said simply.

'But — '

'These gals must be plumb tired of hearing us talk,' Benteen said quickly, nodding at Molly and Miranda. He smiled at the girls. 'When your pa is better I'll show him a good fishing hole I found,' he added. 'So he can take you fishing. Would you like that?' Both girls nodded. They were so sweet and they'd been through enough, Benteen decided. He didn't want them upset by anything they might overhear. Rebecca and Gloria took the hint and Rebecca said, 'I'll get these young ladies situated upstairs.'

Molly scooted from her chair and, gently placing her hand on Benteen's arm, she said, 'Thank you for saving us.' Benteen felt a lump in his throat as they were ushered away. Those were the first words either little girl had spoken to him. Gloria was watching him carefully and Benteen sipped his coffee, doing his best to act calm. He would wait for Rebecca to return before speaking again. A moment later Rebecca once again took her seat and all eyes were on Benteen. The restaurant was strangely quiet.

Benson spoke first. 'What kind of threat can they pose with fifty Nickles riders after them, not to mention every lawman west of the Mississippi?'

'The most dangerous men are the kind that don't quit,' Benteen said. 'These men are killers, and I've upset their plans. There will be a reckoning.'

'What do you propose to do?'

'I propose to make myself a target.'

The silence in the room deepened as all present weighed these words.

'I have my Colt,' Benson said, 'and the Sharps rifle. It's my duty to avenge my wife's murder. You'll not handle this alone.'

Benteen admired Benson's courage, but the man was being foolish.

'The way I see it,' Benteen went on, 'you're still fairly weak. Shrive and Driggs would make you a corpse right quick. Why don't you leave this to me?'

'You're as stubborn as a jug-headed mule,' Benson said. 'But if the opportunity presents itself I'll kill them both.'

'Then I guess I'll have to make certain the opportunity doesn't present itself. I'd hate to see those two pretty gals lose their father, too.'

Gloria was staring intently at Benteen and to him her eyes were bottomless, the curl of her lips suggestive of passions long dormant in them both. It was an odd feeling as he glanced at her, but then he turned away quickly. They had not spoken of that impetuous kiss she had given him, and now here he was explaining that he planned on facing Shrive and Driggs alone. And it was Gloria who spoke next.

'I'd certainly be disappointed if the man who came to my rescue was suddenly killed. I do hope I'm not being forward, Hank.'

He liked the sound of his name when she said it.

'So the way it is,' Benteen said, trying to stay on track, 'is to be alert.'

'Which of the two is the faster?' Benson asked.

'Don't know. But Driggs is crazy as a loon. He's the one to watch. Neither of them will play it straight. It won't be like in those dime magazines, coming straight at you like Hickok did in Missouri.'

'Was that true about Hickok?' Rebecca asked.

'That's the way I heard it,' Benteen said. 'He shot Dave Tuft near the courthouse in Springfield, Missouri, at a distance of a hundred yards.'

'Can you shoot like that?' Benson asked.

'I can hit the target well enough. These Peacemaker Colts are a sight easier to handle than those old Navy models.'

'Some still swear by the Navy Colt.'

'I guess it depends on what you're accustomed to.' Benteen paused. 'It didn't do Wild Bill a bit of good in the end.'

'He was killed ten years ago, I think it was,' Benson said, 'Over in the Black Hills.'

And so the evening waned. The conversation touched many topics and Benteen relished the feelings of goodwill and friendship that were suddenly very much a part of his life. An hour later he bid them all goodnight. Gloria walked him to the door and she touched his arm gently, the way young Molly had.

'Hank, I know this isn't something you want to hear, but please be careful. I know you're a proud man but I just don't want to see you get hurt.'

'Just trust me,' Benteen said and before she could reply he was out the door, instinctively stepping away from the bright doorway. He moved right and crossed over to the side opposite his hotel. If anyone had been watching earlier they'd set a trap and hit at the hotel's door just as he stepped into the light.

He made his way cautiously through

the darkness, pausing occasionally to listen and watch. Again, there was nothing. All the same, he waited thirty minutes to make certain no sharpshooter lurked in the shadows. When he was ready he entered the hotel briskly, pausing only once more, this time outside his door. His Peacemaker was in his hand when he swung the door open. The lamp had burned down but in the faint glow he could see that he was alone.

He locked the door, propped a chair under the handle as an extra precaution, and took off his hat, boots and gunbelt. He blew out the lamp, then, with the gun in his hand, he eased himself on to the bed with a sigh. He was thinking that the wind had blown him along a dusty and meandering trail when he fell asleep.

Outside his window the night breeze picked up but Hank Benteen slept soundly.

10

The dreams of evil men are ripe with greed. Mason Shrive was thinking the best way to hurt a man was to take away something he loves. What did Benteen love? He didn't know, but the man had made friends and they could all die. Nickles and his son Jake would have to die as well, otherwise Shrive himself was a dead man. Accepting that the odds were against him he determined to destroy as many lives as possible. All because they had ruined his plan to make himself wealthy.

Mason Shrive understood greed better than most. His life was predicated upon the quest of selfish pursuits. It would have been so easy to have simply shot Benteen the minute he rode into town. Now his claim on the homesteaders' property was nullified, and Nickles wouldn't rest until he was dead.

He blamed Driggs. That rattle-brained fool would die as well, but that would have to wait. He didn't like admitting it, but he still needed Driggs. If that damn fool could stop himself from going berserk he could help Shrive kill Nickles and Benteen. There was no future for Shrive unless he took care of the elder Nickles and Benteen. Jake Nickles would be less problematic. The kid didn't have any backbone, but Shrive would kill him anyway. He didn't want to take any chances. He had to put himself into a situation where he wasn't looking over his shoulder any longer.

He looked out of the window of the shack where they'd been hiding and cursed. He'd been hiding out for three days — three long days after Driggs had met him here and told him how he'd failed to kill Benteen. But Kendrick was dead. That was the only good news. Kendrick's death meant one less gunman to hunt.

It was hot and dusty in the cabin and

they were getting low on food. Driggs slept soundly on the plank remains of a bed. Shrive resisted the urge to strangle him then and there. Driggs snored loudly, his mouth open, his yellow teeth gleaming in the afternoon light. Perspiration matted his hair to his fat head.

I'd kill a sick dog so why not shoot Driggs now?

Because he wanted an extra gun. Shrive cursed again. He had to nurture whatever fragment of hope he had for survival. Benteen's bullet had only nicked Driggs on the arm. Nickles was formidable and Benteen's reputation gave even hardened men reason to pause. And Driggs was unstable. Shrive worried that if Driggs had one of his 'spells' they were doomed. The man sometimes suffered from what he had once heard a doctor call 'battle fatigue'. Some soldiers suffered from it during the war. For Shrive, it simply meant the damn fool got his brains rattled when an infantry shell exploded near him. Men like Driggs were better off dying from their wounds, but Driggs had beaten the odds and survived.

He went out and smoked while he looked over the valley. They were holed up in an old miner's shack in the foothills of the Big Horn mountains. A day's ride would put them in Pitchstone. Riding east into the Dakotas would only postpone their showdown with Nickles. They had to make a move.

When Driggs woke up a while later Shrive thought it was a good time to act. Driggs sat at the plank table drinking the last of their coffee. His eyes were red and his face gleamed with perspiration.

'It's time to move,' Shrive announced. 'Are you up to riding?'

'What are you planning?'

'We have to go after Nickles and Benteen. By now they must think we rode on. They'll be sending scouts north and south trying to pick up our trail. They'll never expect us to double back.'

'And then what?'

'And then we kill them.'

'Only if I get some time with a woman.'

'What?' Shrive was surprised. 'At a time like this you're thinking about a filly?'

'I want Rebecca Deloney, and maybe the Nash woman.'

Shrive thought it over. 'You'll have to kill Dave Benson right away. And he'll be armed.'

'I'll finish what I started.'

'You have to do it right this time. If you'd done it right the first time we wouldn't be in this fix.'

'Damn your eyes!' Driggs pounded his fist on the table. For a second Shrive thought he would pull his gun and his hand dropped instinctively to his holster.

'Don't you be tellin' me what I need to do!' Driggs hissed. 'You talked me into this fool idea about claiming the homesteaders' ranches and sellin' 'em for grazing rights. Now I wanna get this done. From here on out you just follow me. I'll take care of it all right.'

Shrive knew there was a point where arguing with Driggs was useless so he let it go. 'Then you call it,' Shrive said.

Driggs finished his coffee and tossed the tin cup at the wall. He wiped his mouth with his sleeve.

'We ride in a few hours. We can reach Pitchstone by morning and hole up in back of the dry-goods store. There's an old supply shack ain't bein' used. Then at night we can move about unseen.'

Shrive nodded. It was about what he had planned anyway. 'We have to kill them all and I'll start with Benson,' Shrive reminded him.

Driggs grinned. 'But before we do they'll wish they was dead.'

★   ★   ★

A warm breeze drifted down from the mountains. True to his word Charles Nickles organized a team of freight wagons to begin hauling lumber, logs and supplies to the site of the Benson

194

and Nash ranches. The Benson cabin went up first and on the third day Nickles had his men build a barn, set a corral in place and, last of all, as a personal gesture, they set a white-washed picket fence around Josephine Benson's grave.

Benteen sat astride his new black roan, a new Winchester in the saddle boot. Nickles was a hard but fair man. Benteen couldn't have guessed at this turn of events. He watched from a distance, but was ever alert. There wasn't any sign of Shrive or Driggs. None of the scouts and trackers sent out by Nickles had reported crossing their trail. Benteen believed that was all the more reason to suppose that they were still in the area.

The summer was in full bloom. During the day the fragile sky was piled with drifting clouds and the sun baked the valley. At sunset the world was absolutely still, the orange sun burning between the mountain peaks as the shadows scrambled for a foothold. Each evening Benteen was on horseback about three miles out of town on a small hill. From here he could look northwest into the valley where the new Benson cabin stood, or east where the oil lamps of Pitchstone twinkled in the velvety distance.

One evening Benteen came into town and sat with Nickles in Rebecca's restaurant. In the morning Nickles would have his men begin work on the Nash cabin. The night was still and warm and only Benteen seemed aware of the faint breeze that crept in the open door and helped ease the stifling heat.

'Pride can get a man killed,' Nickles said when they finished eating. 'If this plays out the way you think then Shrive and Driggs won't come straight at you. Have you ever seen how a wounded coyote acts?'

'I have,' Benteen replied. 'A wounded animal can be more dangerous than a healthy one.'

'Precisely. These men aren't smart,

but they have their pride.'

'That's why I've asked Benson to stay in town awhile. It'll be some time before he's back to full strength anyway.'

'Once the Nash cabin is ready I have to pull out. I'll be taking most of my men with me. It's seventy miles to my spread. I can't afford any further distractions, but if you need help just send a rider. It's a full day's ride, but I'll come. I can leave Joe Driscoll. He's as sensible as a man can be. Send him if you need help.'

'I'm obliged.' Benteen said.

Nickles caught Benteen's eye and consulted his drink before continuing. Benteen could sense he was working up to something.

'You said my boy did all right.' It was a statement and not a question. Benteen nodded and waited. Nickles took another drink. 'His mother was too soft for this country. But she taught him how to read and write. He's a lot like her and he's got something of me in him as well. We're not close, and at times I've thought he was plain dumb, but now I see I was wrong. He's just growing up to be a different man.'

Nickles drank and glanced around the room. Benteen suddenly felt like a priest in a confessional. He didn't like the feeling, but Nickles drank steadily and alcohol loosened a man's tongue.

'Sometimes a boy has to make his own mistakes before he becomes a man.' Benteen offered.

'So it is,' Nickles said. 'I saw a lot of killing in the war. Brother against brother. I read in the papers now that it was about abolishing slavery, but that isn't right. It was about preserving the Union. Those damn Southerners got the notion they were better than this thing we call the American dream.'

Benteen took a sip of his own drink, surprised by the turn in the conversation.

'President Lincoln wanted to keep that dream alive and he succeeded. He believed in our Constitution and our Declaration and gave his life for it. That problem with the slaves was a small part of the problem that led those rebels to secede from the Union. The country can't be divided. Maybe those Southerners are just too full of themselves.'

Nickles paused and hacked into the spittoon down near the brass rail. He adjusted himself on his seat.

'I was at Gettysburg. I killed eight rebels that afternoon. The youngest was maybe fifteen. After I shot him he held his belly and tried to stop the blood from bubbling out. He called out to his mother.'

Nickles stared into his glass, his eyes blazing with memories. Benteen didn't tell him he had been present at Hatcher's Run and for an instant he heard the *pop!* of the rifles and the roar of the cannons. Gunsmoke drifted across the years and when he looked at the mirror behind the bar he saw two old warriors trying to drink away the painful memories of their youth. He looked away.

'This problem with the homesteaders can cause another war. We don't need that, but it's bound to happen in Johnson County. There's a point where fighting gets out of control and the killing never stops. This country can't survive that way. So I'll do my bit here to keep the peace.'

Nickles sighed. Benteen thought the man had a lot on his mind but he held a wary admiration for him. But wary because he didn't envy the pressure this man placed on himself.

'I reckon you'll get through this all right,' Benteen said, 'And Jake's finding his way just fine. He'll be an asset to you now.'

Nickles frowned. 'I appreciate hearing that.'

The two men finished their drinks and shook hands without another word. Benteen went out into the sun-filled street and looked at the town. A warm mountain breeze was snaking into town. The breeze did nothing to dispel the heat, in fact, it added to the stifling

200

warmth. The hot, humid air would eat away at them, burning them and forcing them to slow down. The town glimmered like a mirage. Benteen thought he might stay here as Nickles had. It was a good place to put those bitter memories to rest and possibly even build other memories, but the wind also carried a slithering sound like that of a snake shedding its skin. Despite the heat, Benteen shivered.

★ ★ ★

The following morning Benteen sat on a chair outside the restaurant and watched the wagons roll out of town. It would take them three days to build the Nash spread, then Nickles would pull out. Benteen figured they'd wait until Nickles was gone before they came after him. But then he had a second thought as he mulled over his conversation with Nickles.

He'd been avoiding Gloria. When he saw her that morning at breakfast she smiled at him from across the room and his heart fluttered. Her skin was moist and pink in the morning light that fell through the wide window that looked on to the street. The heat was already piling up and Rebecca had propped open the restaurant door, trying to catch a breeze. He smiled at Gloria and she joined him as he ate but they didn't speak. The communication between them now was silent and he appreciated her restraint. The thought crossed his mind that she'd be disappointed if he was killed, and she had said as much. It was the first time in years that his existence had meaning for someone other than himself and he found it disconcerting.

The afternoon dragged on. After lunch he rode out to watch the ranch and barn rising from a distance, making a wide circle around the Nash homestead. The air was still and hot and his new shirt was dripping with perspiration. The valley was quiet. He tried to think what Shrive and Driggs might do next. The only thing he could think of was an ambush. But where?

He recalled Nickles telling him these men weren't smart, but they were like injured coyotes. They would lash out mercilessly. But when? The air brought him the sound of hammers striking nails and the muffled grunts of the Nickles hands putting their backs into their work. He admired the fact that Nickles commanded such loyalty.

He rode back to Pitchstone and found Joe Driscoll leaning against a hitching rail, smoking a thin cigar. Driscoll nodded at Benteen.

'This heat would slow down the devil,' he said.

Benteen came up next to him and leaned against the post. He held his hands gently on his hips as his gaze took in the street. He seemed at ease but alert and Driscoll noticed the way his eyes touched everything.

'Maybe the devil,' Benteen said in response, 'but not Shrive or Driggs.'

Driscoll suddenly felt nervous. 'You think they'll come after you today?'

'Soon. Don't know when.'

Benteen was still watching the street and Driscoll's uneasiness increased.

'I've seen Driggs shoot. He's not all that fast or accurate.' Driscoll paused, glancing at Benteen. 'That night in the saloon I heard what you said about being fast and accurate.'

Benteen shrugged.

'You could easily have killed Jake,' Driscoll continued. 'But in a second you had to make up your mind not to.'

'Killing is nothing to be proud of,' Benteen said.

'Well, things changed mighty quick. Jake is over at the saloon drinking coffee. I heard him tell his pa he'd keep an eye on things and back you up. It's like he's your friend now that you busted his nose.'

Benteen glanced at the saloon. An extra gun couldn't hurt but Jake had more enthusiasm than skill.

'The kid turned out all right,'

Benteen said. 'What do you know about Shrive?'

'Not much. He's a capable drover but not exactly easy to like. He signed on about a year ago.'

Benteen's attention hadn't wavered. As they talked his attention enveloped the street with the same intensity as the heat that settled over the town. Driscoll took off his hat and wiped his brow with a bandanna.

'Could use some coffee myself,' Benteen said. 'But not too hot.' And with that he walked away. Driscoll couldn't help but notice that Benteen walked with his right hand near his gun.

* * *

The red swollen eyes of Walt Driggs followed Benteen as he crossed the street, the breeze ruffling the branches but doing little to ease the heat that lay over the valley like a hot blanket. Sweat dribbled from his unwashed hair and dripped from his nose. His lips trembled. He reclined on the roof of the livery, the blazing eye of the sun burning him alive as his sweat-drenched palm gripped his rifle.

Time and heat had exacted a high tariff from a man for whom peace was something that had been shattered at Gettysburg on that hot day in July when Driggs followed General George E. Pickett in his charge on Cemetery Ridge. By then Driggs had forgotten what the war was about; he only knew the incessant detonation of artillery, the pop of muskets, and the screams of the dying.

What tranquility he had experienced in life only came when he wore socks and boots, for he had been barefoot at Gettysburg, the soles of his feet torn and bleeding, and he'd followed a Georgia boy into a thicket to steal the boots of a dead Union soldier when the Federals opened up with cannons.

He paid little attention to the shouted instructions and reveled in the fact that he once again wore boots as he followed Pickett into history, his right eardrum already shattered and bleeding from an exploding shell.

Pickett, goddamn Pickett. He gripped his rifle. He had to get something from all of this. Money could buy it all. A woman, a home, anything he wanted. But first he had to kill again, and again. Benteen was one man. How many had he killed during the war? He'd lost count. Benteen had been clever when Driggs almost surprised him at the Talbot grave site. Almost. The thought irked him. And Benteen had shot him in the arm. It was only a flesh wound but it hurt like hell.

He was hoping for rain. The heat was too much. The rain would soothe his parched skin. He squinted against the sunlight, particles of dust bursting across his eyes like shrapnel. He could not remember a day when the sun had not burned him, shriveled him. He was becoming a dry husk and he hated himself for it. When he turned his head to mark Benteen's path he thought he might shoot him then, but it was too easy. He wanted Benteen to know it was coming.

Shrive was camped on the edge of town waiting for nightfall. Shrive had made this all happen. Take the land away from the homesteaders. Sell the grazing rights to Nickles. Now Driggs was sitting on a tarpaper rooftop and slowly burning to death.

Then despair washed over him and he went into a convulsion, his fingers loosening their grip on his rifle, the artillery shells again bursting around him, spittle flicking from his lips as his eyes rolled back in his head. When he regained consciousness some time later he stared up at the stars and they appeared like bullet holes in the dark fabric of eternity. He knew with certainty then that the time for killing had arrived.

11

Nightfall only pushed aside the heat, Benteen thought. It still hung over them, but better this than winter. He'd been through enough long winters to appreciate the short, hot summers. Whatever thin breeze that had crept in during the day had disappeared. He stood at the entrance to the alley that ran between the feed and grain store and the livery. He was invisible in the darkness.

An hour ago he'd been sitting in the shadows on the boardwalk outside Rebecca's restaurant when he saw a dark shape moving in the alley. The figure had slinked to the street but retreated before Benteen could identify him. But it didn't matter which one it was.

He thought the man had been on the rooftop. By climbing on to a woodpile,

Benteen was able to lift himself up and peer at the roof. It was empty, but he was convinced one of them had been hiding here. He took his position at the alley's entrance to wait and watch. From this vantage point he could see Rebecca's restaurant and the saloon's batwing doors. A yellow glow backlit the saloon. Rebecca had closed the restaurant for the evening and the door was shut. At his suggestion she had taken to pulling the curtains closed.

After some time he thought he heard a muffled voice from the direction of the restaurant, and then a louder voice followed. He was running instantly, his gun drawn. The flat snap of a rifle shot hammered through the sweltering heat. Dave Benson's Sharps rifle!

He went through the door and into the restaurant in a crouch. He heard their voices in the back. A sense of urgency driving him, Benteen turned the corner and saw Shrive with his hand around Rebecca. Her eyes were wide with fear. Benson had his rifle trained on them but he wouldn't fire again with Shrive using Rebecca as a shield. Gloria was hunched on the floor, tears running down her face.

Benteen raised his gun.

'You won't shoot,' Shrive rasped, 'or this girl dies.'

'Maybe,' Benteen said calmly.

Benson glanced questioningly at Benteen. Holding his Colt steady, Benteen cocked the hammer. The clicking of the cylinder was incredibly loud in the small room. Without taking his eyes from Shrive he said, 'Are the girls upstairs?'

'Yes, they're with Elma,' Gloria said from her prone position.

'He's wounded,' Benson said. 'My shot took him in the side.'

Benteen let his gaze drop to Shrive's shirt and he saw a splatter of blood. Shrive had his gun to Rebecca's head, his thumb on the hammer, his finger tight against the trigger. He thought about how many times he'd practiced with his Colt. Was he fast enough? The shot was easy. He could hit Shrive in the face with one shot. Twenty feet separated them. But would Shrive's gun discharge? It was a gamble he didn't want to take. If Shrive's hand flinched then Rebecca would die. But he couldn't allow Shrive to use her as a hostage. He would certainly kill her. He had to stall for time.

'What were your plans after you killed the homesteaders?'

Shrive stared incredulously at Benteen. 'We had a plan, all right,' Shrive said. 'We could have sold off the grazing rights and made some good money.'

'Nickles would have been suspicious. People would have questioned the sudden disappearance of those homesteaders.'

'It was Driggs who ruined things,' Shrive said. 'He's got something wrong with him. He goes plumb loco, like a rabid dog.'

Benteen shifted his weight from his left foot to his right, an unobtrusive move that set him a millimeter to

Shrive's right. He wanted a better shot, and he had to get Shrive to relax his gun hand just a tad.

'I'll kill Driggs later,' Benteen said. He wanted to keep Shrive talking.

'I've got this gal, now,' Shrive said. 'And you'll be doing as I say!'

'No. I'm going to shoot you,' Benteen said.

Shrive's eyes widened in astonishment. 'To hell you will! You're as loco as Driggs! I've got this woman! Don't you understand me?'

Shrive's voice was high-pitched. He was nearly screaming, his face flushed with anger and fear. The gun dropped a fraction of an inch and Benteen saw his chance. His gun roared but in that instant Shrive flinched and Benteen's bullet creased his head. He screamed and stumbled backwards. Benson dropped the Sharps rifle and flung himself at Rebecca. He pulled her to the ground as Benteen emptied his Peacemaker into the darkness beyond the doorway.

When the gun's reverberation ceased

echoing off the walls Benteen looked around him. 'Is everybody all right?' he asked.

Benson kicked the rear door shut and pulled Rebecca to her feet. They stared at each other a moment and Rebecca trembled violently as Benson held her close.

'We're alive, thanks to you,' Gloria said. 'Did you kill him?'

'No.'

Benteen remained rooted to the spot he'd occupied since firing at Shrive. He flipped open the Colt's loading gate, thumbed the ejector rod and punched out the smoking brass shells. They tinkled harmlessly to the floor and he reloaded using the cartridges in his belt loops. He loaded five and eased the hammer down on the empty cylinder.

'They're going to hit us again,' Benson said. 'They'll try to chip away at us until we're all dead.'

'That's right,' Benteen said. 'Keep that Sharps loaded. I'd carry the Colt, too.'

Rebecca had regained her composure and stared hotly at Benteen. 'That's the last time he puts his hands on me,' she said thickly. She licked her lips nervously. 'I'll keep the Winchester with me from here on out.'

Benteen and Benson exchanged looks. The woman had gumption. Benteen had no doubt she'd never be caught by surprise again. Gloria went up to Rebecca and hugged her.

'I've got a rifle, too,' Gloria said. 'I never expected they'd come in here after us.

'Lock both doors and keep the lamps burning low. Don't open the restaurant for anyone until I come back in the morning.'

'You aren't going after them?' Gloria couldn't hide her surprise.

Benteen frowned but said nothing.

'I'm going with you,' Benson said.

'No, Dave. I need you to stay here. It's going to be a long night. Stay healthy for those two little girls.'

Before Benson could reply Benteen

pulled open the door and stepped into the darkness. He pulled the door closed behind him and a few seconds later he heard the lock click into place. He peered into the darkness. Shrive was out there somewhere, wounded, and waiting to fight.

Benteen didn't like being on the defensive. He would have to take the fight to them. Shrive would be desperate now that he was wounded. He wondered how much damage his bullet had done. He had seen the shot burn across the right side of Shrive's head, just below the eye, clipping the ear. And Benson's shot would mean a loss of blood.

Shrive would be pressed hard to survive the night. But everyone handles pain differently, Benteen thought. Shrive could still make a formidable opponent. And where was Driggs?

He faded into the darkness, heading toward the corral. The gunfire would have alerted Jake Nickles and Joe Driscoll. They would have to fend for themselves until Benteen could reach them. For now, he reveled in the dark night.

The sliver of moon offered little light, but as he approached the corral his eyes had adjusted to the darkness. He could make out the shape of the fence and darker shapes of the horses inside the corral. He dropped to one knee and listened. He heard the dull clop of a hoof as a horse moved, the trilling sound of insects in the underbrush, and distantly, perhaps a mile east, an owl hooted.

Benteen didn't like the idea that Driggs or Shrive might circle around and try to gain entry into the restaurant again. He had to take the fight to them.

He forced himself to remain calm. He stood motionless in the dark, invisible to any prying eyes. Satisfied that no one lurked in the corral, Benteen made his way along the fence-line toward the stockyards. Again he paused and listened but heard only the mooing and grunts of the cattle amongst the usual night sounds. He moved on, plowing into the darkness. He regained the boardwalk on the southern edge of town. He edged himself into the shuttered doorway of the dry-goods store. He didn't believe he'd been spotted, but he would wait here until he was certain.

From this vantage point he could look north and make out the faint light behind the curtain in Rebecca's restaurant. But for the faint glow from a few windows on the north end, the street was blanketed in darkness. The saloon gave off the brightest glow. Light spilled from the doorway and pooled on the street like a yellow mirage that shimmered when the batwing doors were pushed open. While he watched a fat drunk tumbled out of the saloon and made his way to the hotel. He wondered where Jake Nickles and Joe Driscoll were holed up. He strained his eyes peering into the darkness but all he saw were shadows among shadows.

Had he seen a shadow move?

He couldn't be certain. He decided to go around the back. He slid from his perch and darted into an alley, but then he stopped almost immediately. Again, he waited and listened, his eyes straining to see into the impossible blackness. Benteen's senses were finely tuned, and far more sensitive than most men's, but this wasn't a time to make a mistake. One slip-up would cost him his life.

After a short wait he skipped out of the alley and moved stealthily along the back alley. His goal was to come up behind the saloon and enter it from the rear. But the open ground made him feel vulnerable. Only a few shacks and outhouses filled the spaces on his right, otherwise it was all shrubbery and small trees. The perfect place for a man to hide on a night dark as this.

Catwalking with frequent stops to listen, Benteen paused behind the telegraph office. The saloon was next. Yellow light seeped from the rear door. He could hear muffled voices. He inched his way to the next alley, his hand on his gunbutt. He crept up to the saloon door and peered through a crack.

Jake Nickles and Joe Driscoll were drinking coffee with their backs to the rear door, although Driscoll was positioned so that he could cover the rear simply by turning his head. A sawed-off twelve-gauge shotgun rested across his knees. Nickles had his Colt resting on the card-table. Benteen frowned. They were ready. The barman was polishing glasses and looked bored. Two soiled doves were sitting at the table closest to the front door. They were playing cards and looked unhappy. Benteen guessed that two young whores like those would be upset that two young men like Nickles and Driscoll were ignoring them. He had no doubt they'd attempted to ply their trade with the two men. Benteen admired the men's discipline.

But the rear door was the one weakness in their defense. At first Benteen thought he would slip into the saloon and discuss the set-up with them, but he quickly changed his mind. Driscoll had the door covered but it wasn't adequate. Benteen could easily crash through the door and kill both men with two well-placed shots. Still, they had done well, and they weren't gunfighters. Against anyone but Shrive and Driggs they would have a solid chance. But Shrive and Driggs weren't common men, just as Benteen was out of the ordinary.

He decided the best way to help Nickles and Driscoll was by scaring them into realizing their mistake.

If he did this right it would draw attention to the saloon and the alley, so he would have to be fast. He visualized the return route in his mind. The gambit might also draw out Shrive and Driggs, so brevity was key. When he was ready he turned his back on the saloon door, pulled his Peacemaker and fired one shot into the dirt. The sound was thunderous. In the same instant Benteen was running.

He sprinted along the way he had come only moments before, twisting himself into the side alley and stopping. His heart beat loudly in his ears. He had heard the scuffling of boots and scraping of chairs after he fired his shot and he knew that Nickles and Driscoll would be focused on the alley. There was no time to rest. After a moment's pause he cut around to the main street, this time his gun in his hand as he once again slipped into the blackened doorway of the dry-goods store.

He looked toward the restaurant. Shadows among shadows, but something moved across the street, opposite the saloon. A figure had darted into an alley.

So there's one of them, he thought, *now where's the other?*

Now murder was in his heart and he prepared himself. If he killed one of them now it would make the final hunt easier. He thought about that first day when he rode up to the smoldering ruins of the Benson homestead and saw

Josephine dead in the dirt. And he thought about the frightened faces of those two little girls and of the anguish in Dave Benson's eyes.

Time ticked slowly onward and sweat trickled down his face. His hat brim was soaked with perspiration. Good way to break in a new hat, he thought. Chase two killers down a dark street. He thought about Gloria in the restaurant. Gloria breathing heavily from the excitement, a sheen of perspiration across her brow, her hair falling in curls at her shoulders, her mouth partly open as she breathed, her eyes catching the glow of the oil lamp as she watched him earlier. Now Elma would be upstairs with the girls but Dave Benson would be stationed near the kitchen, guns at the ready. Gloria and Rebecca would have their Winchesters at hand. The image made him smile. Now that hell had come to town these two lethal ladies would welcome the devil with a fusillade of lead. Nobody would catch them unawares twice. That restaurant was the safest place in town tonight.

He went left and blended into the darkness of a gully that ran along the south end of town. He followed the gully west until it curled into the foothills. He made his way across a plain of sage and scrub until he arrived at an outhouse. From here he made his way along a row of shacks until he was behind the buildings opposite the dry-goods store. The man hiding in the shadows was up in that area near the feed and grain warehouse.

Benteen realized he was at an disadvantage. He wasn't familiar with the alleys and outlying buildings on this side of town. He would be crossing open ground, visible to any gunman hiding in one of the buildings. And by the time he traveled fifty yards they could have moved, perhaps even returning to their perch above the dry-goods store.

He didn't have any choice. Benteen reached a shack and slipped behind it.

He cursed the lack of wind. There was no sound, no tell-tale footfall to tell him their position. He was like a blind man stumbling through the dark.

But there was something!

His instincts told him that danger was near. He could feel it in the stillness, hear it in the empty spaces. He stepped out from behind the shack, secure in the darkness, but his senses alert. He faced the two-story warehouse and let his eyes and ears probe the depths of blackness. His hand pulled his Colt from the holster and he let his arm dangle at his side, the gun held loosely in his hand.

He would be visible only if he stepped forward, so he stood like a statue amongst the black wall of night. Then something caught his eye and his gaze swept upward. The loft door of the warehouse had moved. At least one man was up on the second level, just inside that door. It was a good position. He could see a long section of the main street through the alley in addition to the restaurant's front entrance.

Benteen calculated the man's position. He would be crouched on one knee at the center of the two hinged doors. He would see Benteen the instant he moved.

In a blur of motion he raised his arm and fired, the Colt spewing flame, and then he stepped behind the shack and waited. The gunshot tore a hole in the silent night, echoing like thunder off the clapboard buildings. A cry of anguish flew across the stillness. Benteen smiled grimly.

He made his way around the gully and came back on to the main street, but this time opposite the dry-goods store. A few yards away stood the barbershop, its doorway recessed about a foot. As he crossed the boardwalk he lifted a wooden chair from its resting place with his left hand and placed it inside the recessed doorway. He sat down and in the darkness, his fingers tracing their way across his gun, he replaced his spent cartridge.

He waited. He knew his shot had struck hard, but was it Shrive or Driggs? At least one of them was seriously wounded. Shrive was already hurt and Benteen's instinct told him that it was Shrive whom he'd hit a second time. From his seat outside the barber's he could see the dry-goods store. It was possible that Driggs had returned to his perch. The man in the feed and grain warehouse would either bleed to death or wait until morning before attempting an escape.

He glanced at the stars. It was past midnight and the long night lay before him. There was nothing else to do. They had nowhere to go unless they decided to saddle up and ride out now. If they did he'd hear them and he'd let them go. They wouldn't be hard to track. But that wasn't going to happen. Driggs would stay and fight. Shrive was probably hurt too badly to make a decision.

Benteen holstered his gun. Each conflict presented its own problems.

Those problems were clear to Benteen. He had to stay awake and alert. At least five long hours loomed before him. And he had to stay alive. Simple, he thought. Just stay alive, and in the morning he would kill the two bad men.

But he knew that nothing was ever as simple as it appeared.

12

There are degrees of darkness. They overlap each other and blend together as do the waves that wash upon a beach. They are connected by their often impenetrable depth, but separated by the faint variations of blackness. The sky was not so much black as it was velvet, awash with a sprinkling of stars that arced ever so slowly as the hours ticked past. The mountains were hulking giants asleep on the horizon. The forest was a tangle of rich darkness that breathed of its own volition, alive with sound, brimming with life.

Pitchstone was a maze of darkness, pooled with shadows. Benteen sat diligently in the dark, a shadow sentry, his eyelids occasionally drooping. But he would not sleep. He had a solitary purpose, a grim and fateful rendezvous that he would not miss. But fatigue plagued him. He felt a lassitude creep into his muscles as he waited; it nagged at him and tried to pull him down into the comfortable world of sleep. He fought against it.

Gradually the darkness opened its shade and the stars slipped into a blue pool. The mountains began to take on contours and the forest revealed its myriad details. Pitchstone came out of a gray mist as the sun began to burn upwards, rising in the east like a beacon.

Still Benteen waited. The first birds began to sing as the world emerged from its black cloak. At six o'clock Jake Nickles and Joe Driscoll emerged from the saloon. Driscoll still had his shotgun. They separated on the boardwalk and stationed themselves thirty feet apart. Both men scrutinized the street and spotted Benteen at the same time. He stood up and watched them. Driscoll nodded and Benteen acknowledged this with a nod of his own.

Benteen crossed the street and met

them on the boardwalk.

'We heard some shooting last night,' Discoll said. 'Out in the alley behind the saloon.'

'That was me,' Benteen admitted. 'Thought I had one of them.' It wasn't the complete truth but it would do. 'And I had one up by that grain warehouse. Might have winged him.'

Benteen looked at Jake Nickles. His eyes were red from being up all night but he appeared alert and ready.

'If one of them is wounded we shouldn't have long to wait,' Jake said.

'No we won't,' Benteen agreed. 'A wounded animal will try anything to rid itself of its pain.'

'I never liked Driggs,' Driscoll said. 'He's got shellshocked from the war. You can't trust a man who goes loco every time a gun goes off. Even horses have more sense than that.'

'I saw it happen to a lot of men,' Benteen said. 'They've got something in them that snaps. Maybe it's not their fault. They get shook by the cannons and it affects their mind.'

'It doesn't matter,' Jake said. 'It doesn't give such men the right to do evil things.'

'No, it doesn't,' Benteen agreed.

'Which one do you think it was you hit last night?' Driscoll asked.

'I don't know for sure, but my feeling was Driggs.' Then Benteen told them how he had wounded Shrive at Rebecca's restaurant.

'So we've got two wounded coyotes to deal with,' Driscoll said. 'I'd sure like to use this scattergun on them now.'

'We won't have long to wait,' Benteen said.

He walked away, leaving them to ponder the events of last night. Benteen once again took a position opposite the saloon.

Ten minutes later Charles Nickles emerged from the hotel. He looked at his son and Joe Driscoll before turning his head and setting his gaze on Benteen.

A horse whinnied from an alley. The

sound had been near the feed and grain warehouse. At that moment Dave Benson came out of the restaurant, holding his Sharps rifle. Benteen was relieved that Gloria and Rebecca had chosen to remain inside.

The clip-clop of a horse's hoofs drifted on the morning breeze. Nickles and Driscoll set their sights on the alley opposite them. Benteen began walking toward them, keeping to the left. He was closing the gap when Walt Driggs spurred his horse from the alley. The horse galloped into the street and Driggs, seeing the men, pulled the reins and turned his horse in a circle. He eyes blazed with pain and fury. A red stain was visible on his shirt. So it had been Driggs in the loft last night, Benteen thought.

Nickles and Driscoll went out together and waited in the street. Driggs watched them, his lips trembling. He held a rifle at a downward angle. The first thing Benteen noticed was how much Driggs had changed. He seemed diminished in some way, and he now looked like a man who was shrinking in on himself. His arrogance was replaced by a hollowness; his features were gaunt and his eyes were flat. He appeared to Benteen as a man who had come to realize he was lost.

'You son of a bitch!' he hissed at Benteen.

Dave Benson came up behind Driggs and said, 'Driggs.' As Driggs turned Benson shot him. The bullet ripped through his ribs. He shrieked and raised his rifle to fire as Jake Nickles pulled his Colt and shot him again. Still he refused to relent. Driggs curled his lip in disgust and his flat eyes shone briefly with a desperate anger. For the briefest moment time seemed to stop. Then Driggs was swinging the rifle up and firing, but his horse bucked and the shot slammed into the dirt at Benteen's feet. Driggs was intent on Benteen now, ignoring the other men. With his horse whinnying in fear and bucking, Driggs let go of the reins and pulled his six-shooter with his other hand. Benson was reloading as Nickles fired again, his bullet slamming Driggs from his saddle.

Benteen had come to halt not twenty feet from Driggs as the man was slowly brought to justice before him. His hand hung loosely at his side but he still had not pulled his gun. There was no need. Nickles, Driscoll and Benson advanced on Driggs who lay writhing in the street.

His tongue licked at his dry lips, his yellow teeth gleaming with blood. His Colt and Winchester lay in the dirt at his side. A convulsion shook his body. Shaking violently, Driggs flailed his arms.

'He needs to be put out of his misery,' Jake Nickles said.

But none of them raised his gun while Driggs suffered through his convulsion. At last his eyes rolled back into his head and his eyelids closed. He blinked several times. When he opened his eyes a moment later he stared at Benteen.

'I'm going to kill you,' he said softly.

As he reached for his rifle Nickles, Benson and Driscoll raised their guns and fired. The triple volley echoed off the storefronts and a cloud of dust burst around Driggs as the slugs punched into his chest. His body convulsed once more, then became still.

Charles Nickles made his way across the street and stared down at the blood-soaked body of Walt Driggs. He lit a cigar and blue smoke trailed after him. He looked at his son and said, 'Well done.' Then he nodded at Benson and Driscoll before striding back to the hotel.

But it's not finished yet, thought Benteen, there's one more.

As if predestined to act in this fashion, the wind curled up and ceased moving. The air was hot and heavy. Sweat trickled down from under Benteen's hat. He stared at the clapboard buildings and past them at the primordial past, at the savage wilderness that the frontiersmen had cut and honed until the origins of this town had been carved from the raw land; he saw the future they were attempting to build, the traffic of commerce and industry that would help the ranchers and townspeople thrive, and he knew that once the danger was past this beautiful place would nurture the men and women who loved each other under the indigo sunsets, the insects trilling in the underbrush, the sound of trees being nudged by the wind like a song they could rely on to ease their pain during the long days of toil.

And as quickly as Benteen had these thoughts he brushed them aside. He let his mind flood with an iron resolve and he felt his old confidence return as his finely honed senses took in everything around him.

Shrive was watching. But from where?

He put himself in Shrive's place and thought he would take the high ground like a good soldier. They had all survived the war because they had learned their lessons well.

Take the high ground and cut them down from above. His eyes swept across the rooftops.

Driscoll and young Nickles dragged the body out of the street. Benteen sauntered away, sweat dripping from his face. Keeping to the boardwalk he retraced the path he'd taken the night before. He went to the shack where he'd fired on Driggs in the loft and then on toward the loft itself, where he stood motionless as he thought through the problem. Shrive was wounded and by now his head would be thundering with pain. The bullet had neatly creased his skull last night. He might have gone off to either heal or to die. No, he wouldn't die that easily. He would come at him straight on.

Then get on with it, you bastard!

A dog barked in the distance. The heat seemed to mock him, inviting him into its languid jaws, whispering to him to relax, sit down, wipe the sweat from his face. Take your eyes off the building, take your mind off your problems. Benteen knew that many travelers had perished in the desert because they allowed the heat to dictate its terms. But he wouldn't relent.

Then a man's silhouette filled the patch of sunlight before him and he realized he'd been caught facing the sun. Benteen cursed at himself. Mason Shrive was smoking and calmly watching him. His spurs jangled loudly as he shifted his weight, his hand thumbing back the Peacemaker's hammer, the barrel stabbing flames and smoke even as Benteen was moving.

Benteen was quick and dodged behind an outhouse as bullets thunked and snarled into the planks, whizzing past him. He dove, Colt in hand, and fired once through the wall in the direction where Shrive had been standing. It was a deflection meant only to make Shrive hesitate. Benteen accepted he wouldn't be lucky enough to kill Shrive that easily.

He was up and running, circling the

large grain warehouse. He heard Shrive curse.

'Damn you to hell!' Shrive screamed. 'Keep runnin', old man. I'm gonna bury you soon enough!'

Shrive's gun barked and a slug blasted through the wood, so close to his cheek that he could feel the heat it spent as it passed him. He fired four quick rounds through the wall of the warehouse and then sprinted to the next building. He reloaded. Endless seconds seemed like minutes to him as he punched out the spent shells and thumbed fresh cartridges into the cylinder.

He silently counted to ten before yelling out, 'Come on, you ugly bastard! I'm waiting here!'

Benteen swung around a corner, only to find the street empty. Shrive was hiding.

To his right a pistol boomed and a slug tore at his feet as he saw Shrive in his peripheral vision. Benteen spun and fired twice, smoke wafting from his gun's barrel. He blinked against the stinging sunlight and Shrive was gone.

Benteen retreated behind an outlying building, breathing heavily, his breath short. His lungs heaved and his temples throbbed. Damn Shrive!

He forced himself to remain still. He wasn't going to make the mistake of getting caught with the sun in his eyes a second time. He scrubbed his bristled jaw with one hand as he thought about Shrive getting the drop on him. That never would have happened ten years ago. Was he getting soft or just old? Hell, it didn't matter, he decided. He'd be just as dead if he didn't change his thinking.

Benteen still felt that he had the advantage. Driscoll and young Jake Nickles would be out near the saloon, alert and guns ready. He had to force Shrive to make his play or somehow get him out in the street. It didn't really matter who killed him, only that he die soon.

Benteen bolted from his hiding-place, backtracking to the south, and

241

away from the open lane where the sun burned so hotly over the place that had almost become his grave. He ran at a crouch, his eyes peeled for any sign of Shrive. He had reached the southern-most building when a bullet slammed into the wall six inches from his head. Another shot rang out, sailing over Benteen's head.

Shrive was behind him on horseback and galloping in his direction. Benteen's arms felt like they were tied down with iron ore. He raised his six-shooter and fired, the gun bucking in his hand like an angry mule. Flame belched from the muzzle and the horse reared on its hind legs but Shrive held on.

Suddenly the street was pandemonium. He heard voices along with the echo of their gunfire and he realized Driscoll and Nickles were running in his direction. Benteen swirled about and waved his hands.

'No! Hold your ground!'

They stopped in their tracks. Benteen

was turning and firing again just as Shrive pulled the trigger. The bullet clipped Benteen's thigh, burning like a hot iron. It was a superficial albeit painful wound and he fired again, but Shrive spurred his horse into a gallop. By God, the man was a damn fool!

Shrive had holstered his Colt and pulled his Winchester from the saddle boot as he galloped toward Benteen. The galloping thunder of the horse's hoofs echoed like artillery fire off the storefronts as Shrive leaned to the right in his saddle while lifting the rifle with his left hand and snapping a useless shot at Benteen as he swept past.

Then Shrive whipped the rifle by its large looped lever, making the rifle spin in a complete circle, ejecting the spent brass and slapping another round into the breech. He reined his horse to a halt and fired at Driscoll and Nickles as they scampered away. Shrive had come up near the saloon. He was trapped.

Driscoll and Nickles were forced across the street by Shrive's bold move.

They hunkered down in an alley. Benteen took stock of the situation in an instant and reloaded his gun. When he snapped the loading gate closed he turned as Shrive fired. The slug cut into Benteen's left side. Then Shrive blasted shots in the direction of Driscoll and Nickles before turning his attention back to Benteen. The sudden outburst forced Benteen to dive into an office as Shrive sent bullets slapping into the clapboard front.

Benteen crashed through the doorway, dove to his right, drawing his gun. Then Shrive lost control of his horse which bucked fiercely as he fired. He levered the rifle with his left hand while attempting to shoot Benteen with the Colt in his right hand. It was no good. He was falling from the saddle as Dave Benson came up out of the dusty street and in one fluid motion snapped a bullet into Shrive's side.

Shrive screamed and dropped to the ground but to Benteen's surprise he managed to hang on to both guns.

Benteen emptied the Colt but Shrive was already moving, diving for cover in the alley. Benson came into the storefront and looked at Benteen.

'I'll finish him. You need a doctor.'

'Not a chance. This is the last dance.'

He pulled himself to his feet.

'You truly are a stubborn man,' Benson said.

Benteen punched out the spent brass and reloaded.

He looked out at the street. Nickles and Driscoll were off on the left. Shrive was in the street, a wet red stain on his shirt. He stepped backwards, groggily, like a man on a drunk, but kept his rifle pointed at the doorway. A soft chuckling escaped from Shrive's throat, followed by a faint gurgling and wheezing sound.

'I'll see you in hell, Benteen! You and that damn Driggs!' His voice was utterly cold.

When Benteen peered around the corner again Shrive kept him at bay by firing once in his direction. Nickles and

Driscoll suffered the same treatment when they attempted to fire on Shrive from behind the water trough. In this manner Shrive moved down the street until he stood at the hitching rail in front of the saloon. He propped the rifle against the rail and reloaded his Colt. Then he leaned against the hitching post and decided he had a scorching thirst. He had been thirsty a long time, since he'd ridden into this damnable town with Driggs, and by God he was tired of being thirsty.

He stumbled on to the boardwalk and pushed himself through the batwing door. The barman was just inside the doorframe, watching. Shrive realized he'd left the rifle outside, but no matter, he still had the Colt. He palmed it slowly, rasping at the barman. 'One drink! And a tall one!'

The barman stepped back slowly, shrugged, and made his way behind the bar where he poured Shrive a thick slug of whiskey in a tall glass. The smell of whiskey, kerosene, and tobacco made

Shrive suddenly nauseous and he reeled slightly, tottered forward and leaned heavily against the bar. His boot knocked a spittoon. He watched it roll across the slatted floorboards, clanging to a stop against a table leg.

He turned his head and his eyes fixed on the massive oil painting on the wall behind the bar. The voluptuous woman swathed in silk on an opulent couch stared past him, uncaring. The pain in his gut was sharp and he felt his blood trickling down his abdomen.

He sipped the whiskey. 'I can't pay you right now,' he said to the barman. 'But after I kill Benteen I'll pay you with his money.'

'Forget it. That drink's on the house, pardner,' the barman said. 'I don't collect from dead men.'

Shrive peered intently at the bartender as if trying to fathom the meaning behind his words. He finished the whiskey and slammed the glass on the bar. He checked his gun and turned toward the door. They should be out there about now, he thought, those dumb bastards. He walked slowly to the batwings and looked out. It was hot in the street. His mouth tasted bitter, like a copper coin. Benteen was waiting in the street and Joe Driscoll and Jake Nickles were behind him. Dave Benson was across the street with the rifle, waiting under an awning.

Shrive slipped into the sunlight and strolled casually into the dusty street. Stopping about thirty yards away, he faced Benteen.

'I don't reckon this is the way I planned it.' Shrive's voice was calm.

'I expect not,' Benteen said.

'Let's dance, you old fool!'

Benteen was pulling his gun. Before he had it levelled he felt the impact of Shrive's bullet as it creased his ribs. A second later he was aware of the sound of Benson's rifle thundering in the hot, still air. A flock of sparrows flapped skyward as the gun's retort echoed off the storefronts.

Shrive rocked on his feet and pulled

the trigger, but he never raised his gun completely and the bullet sent up a cloud of dust. A choking wail of anguish rose from his throat. Benteen's gun rapped out a shot and Shrive was falling back, one leg bending quickly. He tottered like a chair with a broken leg, then the other leg bent and he was on his knees in the dust, his heart pumping the blood out of the holes in his chest. He fell face down in the dirt.

Benteen holstered his gun and waited for the dust to clear. Shrive lay dead in the street. Benteen took off his hat and wiped the sweat from his brow, squinting against the sunlight. He let his gaze stray to the hazy line of green hills. He watched the hills for a full minute but there were no answers there. The wind stirred, bringing him the smells of fresh earth and blooming flowers, and ever so faintly, the smell of death.

In his peripheral vision he saw Rebecca and Gloria coming out of the restaurant, and Jake Nickles walking toward his father. Benson went toward

Rebecca; he saw her take Dave Benson's hand. Driscoll followed after Nickles and for an instant Benteen was alone in the street. He was suddenly very tired. But not alone, he thought, I have these dead men for company. He looked around for Gloria but she had disappeared.

Benteen listened to the sound of the trees swaying in a gentle breeze. The branches made a rustling sound that at times sounded like someone whispering in the sunlight. He was conscious of this sound and often felt that it belonged to him alone, although the Sioux understood this sound as well. He set his palm against his side and it came away wet with blood. Not a fatal wound, he thought, but his ribs would hurt like hell for some time. He saw the future clearly and he was filled with a sense of satisfaction. Rebecca would look after Dave Benson and his girls until one day Dave would notice her as if for the first time, and their future would be sealed.

He looked down at the street where his shadow fell into the dust. His shadow stretched up to Gloria's horse. So the old Sioux medicine man had been right.

Gloria looked at him and smiled. 'Let's go take a look at the new cabin together and I'll patch up that hole in your side.'

'It'll be nice to stay out of the wind for a while,' Benteen said.

Gloria nodded and cantered her horse around, leading Benteen's new roan. Benteen grabbed the reins and took a breath.

'You're a good horse,' he said to the roan.

'A man who talks to horses is either wise or foolish, depending on your point of view.' Gloria said with a chuckle.

'So I've been told.'

Hank Benteen reached for the saddle's pommel, stuck his boot in a stirrup, and pulled himself on to his horse. They rode out of town with the wind at their backs.

We do hope that you have enjoyed reading this large print book.

Did you know that all of our titles are available for purchase?

We publish a wide range of high quality large print books including:
Romances, Mysteries, Classics
General Fiction
Non Fiction and Westerns

Special interest titles available in large print are:
The Little Oxford Dictionary
Music Book, Song Book
Hymn Book, Service Book

Also available from us courtesy of Oxford University Press:
Young Readers' Dictionary
(large print edition)
Young Readers' Thesaurus
(large print edition)

For further information or a free brochure, please contact us at:
Ulverscroft Large Print Books Ltd.,
The Green, Bradgate Road, Anstey,
Leicester, LE7 7FU, England.
Tel: (00 44) **0116 236 4325**
Fax: (00 44) **0116 234 0205**

Other titles in the
Linford Western Library:

UNSIGNED AVENGER

John Davage

When Will Cord is shot dead for the brutal killing of Ali Toombs, Joe Hayes and his two sons know the real killer is still at large . . . Could it be Cole Sanderson — a newcomer to Consolation? Saloon girl Maggie Brown knows he's not who he says he is. Or could it be Lew Rosen, editor of the *Gazette*, who suspects the Hayes brothers? Fear and suspicion spread like a prairie fire — is anyone safe from accusation and violence?

FAITH AND A FAST GUN

Chap O'Keefe

Joshua Dillard, the ex-Pinkerton detective, on a sentimental journey to a mission graveyard in Texas, had ridden into trouble. Guns blazed around the headstones as he intervened to save a girl called Faith from the clutches of Lyte Grumman and his gunhawks. Grumman, a cattle baron, believed that a rigged poker game had lost him a thousand head of longhorns. Now he was intent on recouping his loss, whatever it took — and Joshua's Colt Peacemaker was hopelessly outnumbered . . .

GUNS OF PONDEROSA

Chuck Tyrell

When Nate Cahill and his gang take over the town of Ponderosa, sawmill magnate Fletcher Comstock sends for his friend Matt Stryker. However, Cahill is waiting for him. He gelds Stryker's fine Arabian stallion and beats him terribly. But Stryker will not give up. He pins on the marshal's badge, tames a rowdy town and gets rid of the ruthless Cahill gang. Now the guns of Ponderosa blaze and blood runs red in the Arizona high country.

DEATH RANGE

Elliot Long

Bullet-scarred Jack Cain, through with cleaning up gun-crazy ranges and wild cow towns, heads for Montana to buy a small spread and raise cows. But a hundred miles up country, he encounters nine-year-old Ethan Wilder whose ma is shot and near to dying. Will he come and take a look? Reluctantly he agrees, only to find himself ambushed in a hail of bullets — but what follows next turns out to be Jack Cain's greatest test — but can he survive it?